PORT TROPIQUE

All Black Lizard titles are available direct from the publisher or at your local bookstore.

Watch out for the Black Lizard!

PORT TROPIQUE

by Barry Gifford

Introduction by Ed Gorman

Black Lizard Books
Berkeley • 1986

Typography by QuadraType.

Introduction copyright © 1986 by Edward Gorman.

This Black Lizard Books edition published 1986.

Library of Congress Cataloging in publication data:

Gifford, Barry, 1946—
    Port Tropique.

    (A Black Lizard Book)
    I. Title.

PZ4.G4583Po [PS3557.I283] 813'54 80-15440

ISBN 0-88739-012-9

for
El Gringo Grande
and
El Hombre Derecho
and for
Don and Chris

"He had no future. He disdained it. He was a force.... Nobody looked at him. He passed on unsuspected and deadly, like a pest in the street full of men."

—Joseph Conrad, *The Secret Agent*

"Words, as is well known, are the great foes of reality."

—Joseph, Conrad, *Under Western Eyes*

INTRODUCTION

by Edward Gorman

"Death, thought Franz, is the most fascinating thing there is. A friend he'd had in London when he was eighteen, Sullivan Leybourne, had more than anything else in the world wanted to know what it felt like to kill another man."

Arguably these two thoughts—the notion of one's own death and inflicting death on another—form the central obsession of Barry Gifford's remarkable post-*noir* novel *Port Tropique*.

Though it was widely celebrated when it first appeared in 1980, too many critics understood *Port* too quickly.

"This place is a good setting for a movie. All it needs is Hoagy Carmichael instead of the jukebox."

"The music would certainly be better. They made *Treasure of the Sierra Madre* around here. Did you ever read any of B. Traven's books?"

"No, who was he?"

"A German who lived here for forty years, most of it in the bush."

While Gifford's novel invokes many cinematic and literary references, none seems so appropriate to the book itself as the mysterious B. Traven and his doomed

Treasure, for the novel's protagonist, Franz Hall, is a quintessential Traven character.

We might almost concoct a list of Travenesque qualities Gifford imposes on Hall: he is paranoid, guild-ridden, a failure and trapped in the midst of a hopeless situation that may cost him his life (the novel concerns, in part, smuggling in Latin America).

Yet there are differences: Hall is not so iconic as Traven might have painted him. No, he is unmistakably of the American middle classes, in some respects open and familiar. He speaks constantly of literature and movies; of neuroses and social style; and of irony. He is a hipster of the ironic. Nobody would accuse Fred C. Dobbs of that.

But his familiarity is also his mystery. He should be courting beauties in discos, or hanging out with Hollywood writers who speak too glibly of existence. He might have been an actor; he calls himself a writer. Why, instead, is he in the jungle risking his life?

"Even in Port Tropique Franz preferred the poorer neighborhoods and the company of bums and wondered why after all this time one thing did not matter very much more than any other."

So Hall accepts his fate and without begrudging it. Gifford tells us: "If he ever wrote a book, Franz decided, he would put into it everyone he had ever liked or disliked. It would be called *Tragic Creatures*."

Fixated this way, what is the point of struggle?

"A Douglas Fairbanks-like, as well as look-alike, adventurer, Franz's Uncle Buck had been an interesting man."

In many respects Gifford is as playful as Borges. And, like Borges, when he uses a cinematic (or literary) reference, Gifford is being not sentimental (as lesser writers would be) but argumentative. He revises the meaning of accepted images and makes them his own.

Thus, Franz's Uncle Buck, while reminding people of Douglas Fairbanks, is anything but what Beverly Hills' favorite tennis partner had been—Uncle Buck is, in his way, tormented and aimless as Franz himself. If Uncle Buck is iconic at all, it is in the way Jack Kerouac made men iconic. Uncle Buck and Kerouac would have had many good drunks together. The real Douglas Fairbanks would have asked Uncle Buck to shine his shoes.

"In the last few days Franz had thought of everyone he had ever known that he could still remember. The common theory is that when you die your entire life passes in front of you during that final instant. If that was true, it seemed to Franz, then he was dying in slow motion."

So we return to death, "the most fascinating thing there is," and we return to it through the vehicle of memory, for that is what Franz cannot escape. He is cancer-shot with recollections of failure—with his wife, his son (was he really responsible for his son's death?), his parents, his relatives, his friends. He is a target for his own memory, nothing blocks it out. "There was little point to life, he felt, if there was no controlling at least some part of it."

Barry Gifford has given us a fine-tuned little suicide note that has nerve enough to mock itself while being mercilessly serious.

While its form and style owe small debts to everybody from Hemingway to Camus, Celine to Stephen Crane, *Port Tropique* is indivisibly Gifford's own utterance, and a fine and important and lasting utterance it is.

Edward Gorman is the author of the novels *Rough Cut* and *New, Improved Murder;* he co-edits the magazine *Mystery Scene.*

The first thing was the sky, how wide it was and how many clouds there were in it. There were many clouds and every five minutes one of them would block out the sun for as long as a minute and it would still be hot but without the glare. The sun was very hot, it burned you even if you were already deeply tanned. When your back was turned it came into your shoulder blades and felt like the heat was coming from the inside out.

Beautiful Indian girls passed on the street. It was impossible to guess their ages except that they were very young, between fourteen and twenty. Their wide eyes looked at you for a moment very seriously then turned away suddenly and completely.

Franz sat in the zócalo and walked around the town like it was all a dream. He drank beer and ate onions and peppers in the bars by the market where men fell over dead drunk on their faces on the floor. He bargained for whatever he wanted to buy and didn't buy if he didn't feel the price was as low as he wanted to pay and didn't feel badly later because he hadn't bought something.

It rained furiously for a few minutes every day and late at night the wind shook the birds from the flamboyana trees.

He had need to get away, though he'd never had any great love for the tropics. As a boy in New Orleans the heat had seemed unbearable, he'd never gotten used to it, but now it soothed him, and he was beginning to like it.

Walking along the beach at madrugada, the hour just before dawn, companion only to darting lizards and the waves, Franz awoke in a dream where everything was purple, gray, black, invisible.

The large stranger said nothing the entire time. The thin one told Franz someone would meet him tomorrow or the next day, perhaps the day after that, or the day after, here in the zócalo, at this time, and tell him what to do.

Franz was going to ask the thin man why he couldn't be more specific about the date but decided against it. As they walked away from him Franz watched the big guy. He leaned to his left and every few steps spit to the right. Both of the men wore panamas. Franz was certain the big one carried a gun. There was no other reason for a big ugly goon to be wearing a sport coat when it was a good hundred degrees at ten o'clock in the morning.

He ordered a Superior and immediately a citizen came up and grinned and offered his hand and said something unintelligible meaning would Franz buy him a beer too. The people in Port Tropique were handsomer than in the rest of the country. Indian faces spread almost completely around the bowl-like head with eyes that looked straight at you only when you weren't looking or when they were asking for something.

Franz and his new friend drank their beers and sweated and listened to three compañeros sitting at a table play guitars and sing. They were off-key and drunk and the music sounded as bad as the bar smelled. There was a tiny old man sleeping on the floor of the urinal next to the bar but nobody bothered him when they used it, pissing over his body so that only the last few drops fell on him.

A young boy came through the swinging doors wheeling a cart filled with empty bottles. He and the bartender jabbered back and forth for a few minutes before the bartender gave him some money and a bottle of beer. The boy's teeth were very brown and he had a very skinny but muscular body. After he drank the beer he wiped his face with a black rag he kept tucked into his sleeveless shirt under his arm, insulted the bartender and everybody in the bar and went out with his cart.

Franz sat in the zócalo across from the side of the foun-tain where the swishes hung out. If there weren't so many babies he would have been convinced the entire country was queer. Every so often one of the pompadours turned toward Franz and said in a loud voice, "Do you like to dance with me?" or "Do you like homosexuals?"

Early evening was the best time for sitting in the zó-calo. You could watch the sun fall behind the church and the girls going home or to the shops. All of the girls wore crucifixes of course and Franz thought about fucking them on the cool stone floor of the big church while their bent little mothers and grandmothers genuflected and prayed and agonized.

The man reminded him of a snake, the way he twisted his neck and head around as he spoke, squirming his body and looping his arms through the spaces in the bench. His name was Renaldo, he said, but Franz privately labeled him El Serpiente.

"You will bring to the old dock at eight-fifteen the empty suitcase. Nada mas. That's all you have to know. Nada mas. Entiende?"

After El Serpiente had disentwined himself from the bench and walked away Franz considered the danger of the situation. Until now he hadn't really given it much thought, at least as much thought as he now considered he should give it, but seeing this serpent person made it very clear that death was a genuine possibility.

Lying in the bottom of a ravine, the body of his eight-year-old son pinned dead to his chest underneath the wreckage, he had had a moment to consider it, but then he had lost consciousness and now there had been the intervening years to cloud the head. He remembered driving around the curves drunkenly, cursing, the boy silent, then, just before the fall, the large orange moon and his thought of Li Po's attempt to embrace it.

"Please allow my excuse. I am no an Indian. I am work for this bank—" the man was pointing to a business card. "I am officer of this bank. I would like me introduce me to you."

The fat, drunk, stupid officer of a bank who was not an Indian swayed and grinned hopefully at Franz. Franz saw some paper money on the ground by the man's right foot that must have dropped out when he'd taken out his card.

"You dropped something," said Franz, and left the officer of a bank who was not an Indian staggering around by the bench looking for it.

A red and white 1941 Willits school bus squealed around the corner like a fat lady singing opera. Franz watched it zoom down the narrow street scattering citizens and even more recklessly careen around another corner coming as close to turning over as was possible without actually doing so. There were certainly more distressing facts of life in Port Tropique than berserk bus drivers but whenever Franz narrowly avoided being banged down by one that had headed full throttle for him and any other pedestrians unfortunate enough to have cause to undertake the crossing of a road he had a difficult time remembering what they were.

Because of the new laws against the killing of elephants there was a shortage of African ivory and the Japanese had to get horn from North America, from Canada and Wyoming and Montana. Bighorn sheep, elk, moose, caribou, boar and deer were processed there, taken by truck to Tampa, ferried across the gulf to Port Tropique, transferred there and taken by freighter to the Far East, where the tusk and horn became costume jewelry, religious medals, chess pieces, assorted trinkets, then exported legally back across the ocean. Franz had once bought a Japanese-made "genuine ivory" backscratcher in a discount store in San Francisco, but he couldn't remember now what had happened to it.

All he had to do was bring the suitcase, let them fill it, keep it for about twenty-four hours, then deliver it to the others, who would pay him for his services.

Franz looked down from the window at Calle Cincuenta Ocho. In the middle of the street a man was lying under the front end of a 1937 Cadillac fixing something. A woman and several children stood around waiting, also in the middle of the street. All of them were barefoot except for the man.

He went tropical, like any white man queer for both whisky *and* Indians does. Nothing fancy or unusual about it, except he had a wife who stayed with him, and that's always unusual.

Franz was in The Habana, a Spanish-style café off the zócalo where the waiters wore white shirts and black bow-ties and old world politeness was expressed in no way more succinctly than by the ornate ceiling fans that revolved so as not to disturb even the large blue flies that slept on the blades. He was sipping coffee con leche while listening to a Norte Americano professor who was an expert on the local culture and was in Port Tropique on holiday tell with much flourish and an equal amount of undisguised relish the story of another Norte Americano professor, now dead, who had been an expert on the local culture and had gone native and come to a bad end.

The problem for the professor who was not dead and who was telling the story, as Franz saw it, was that the professor who had gone bad and was now dead was also more famous, having made several important archaeological discoveries before achieving the state of disgrace, if only in the eyes of his academic colleagues. Not the least of the sins of the deceased and disgraced professor, according to the professor who was alive and apparently in academic favor and who was telling the story, was his having been memorialized as a figure of semi-mythic proportions by the members of the local culture on which he had been an expert.

"That was poor Max's undoing, that great white father crap," the professor whose name meant nothing to Franz told his informal audience who were seated along the two white tablecloth-covered tables against the back wall of the café.

There were six of them including the two tourist couples from San Antonio and Mobile who were staying at the Hotel Tropique, and Franz and the professor who was drinking tequila cocktails while he bad-mouthed the famous dead man Maximilian Kroner. It is a mistake to be famous while you are alive, thought Franz, but it is an even bigger mistake to be famous after you are dead and be unable to have the pleasure of ignoring your detractors.

"Max Kroner came over from Germany and went to work for an American oil company exploring new territory. They sent him down here—he was just a young man then, twenty-two years old—and he fell in love with the jungle. Being out with sweating mules and poison snakes and billions of stinging insects in the hellhole heat, that's what Max liked. That's when he stumbled on the Esperanza ruins, working for the oil people. It wasn't until later that he went to Harvard and started drinking. He came back here to die, and lasted another twenty years and became a great man. 'El Max' the Indians call him."

"What happened to his wife?" the wife from Mobile asked. "Is she still alive?"

The professor drank down his tequila cocktail and nodded. "Yes, she's still here. Frau Kroner has a large house on the road toward Domingo City, but she doesn't like visitors unless they're locals. She has a lot of family money."

Franz finished his coffee con leche and excused himself. It was late and he did not want to hear the professor start in with the wife from San Antonio and the wife from Mobile about the wife of the dead hero of the Indians.

Franz never saw the rats, but in the morning there were always fresh droppings around the sink. He had learned not to keep any packets of food out, to always keep them in a tightly sealed jar, but in the morning there were always the rat pellets, as if they expected he would slip up one night and forget to replace the remaining biscuits in the jar. Or maybe it was just that they would come and stare into the jar, trying to figure out a way to liberate the contents.

Liberate was a large word in the country, Franz noticed. Or *libertad*, to be more precise. Liberty. The government never admitted there were rebels in the jungle but sent troops regularly on search-and-destroy missions and kept patrols on constant duty in the Montejo section where the rich people lived. Some families, Franz was told, kept large houses just to have parties in and lived in other large houses.

Franz hoped there would not be a revolution while he was there because the government allowed the smuggling operations to continue so long as they were given a percentage of the action. A new government would just mean that there would be a suspension of activity until a new deal could be worked out, but Franz could not afford the time.

After I make enough to leave let them have it, he thought. Let them drag the ones with the refrigerators out of their houses on the Calle Montejo and shoot them or hang them up by their feet or their thumbs like they did to Mussolini and brand them and let las viejas pinch and bite them and scratch them until they bleed. Let them pretend there will never again be a privileged few who keep large houses just to have parties in only let it be after I am somewhere that I can read about it in the newspapers.

He recalled a time when he was a very young boy walking home from grammar school and got lost cutting through a strange yard where a woman was hanging out her wash. Running under the yellow and white sheets and blankets he had been afraid the woman would make fun of him for losing his way. It never occurred to him that she might take him for a thief. When his mother asked him why he was late Franz had cried and been unable to answer.

Once in New York Franz had heard a news report on the radio about how the Turban Saints and the Abyssinian Royal Nomads had rumbled in the Red Hook section of Brooklyn. Three persons were killed and the several injured were taken to such-and-such hospital. Like the results of a football game. It was always a shock to learn of the existence of worlds other than his own.

His grandfather's suitcase would do. It was all leather and covered with stickers from a dozen exotic places and had straps and was large enough to hold it even if it was mostly small bills. This was the suitcase Franz had carried around the world, or most of it, and if something was going to happen that wasn't so good it would help to have an old friend along. He was sure his grandfather wouldn't mind, not only because he was dead but because he had never minded a little scrape.

His grandfather had been an unpredictable man. He'd once been supposed to meet his wife and daughter, Franz's mother, for a holiday in Miami but instead boarded a liner in Boston and sailed to France. He'd wired them from mid-ocean saying he'd changed his mind and would see them back in New Orleans in six weeks.

At first Franz thought he would take the five-shot Ridgefield .38 but changed his mind and took the Smith & Wesson .32 because it was the gun his brother had used on those jockeys in LA and would be more likely to not freeze up in a spot if only for sentimental reasons.

The last time Franz had seen his brother they were out at the Sea Breeze restaurant on the Gulf of Mexico. The guy at the table in front of them had just slumped nose first into his soft-shelled crab, the redhead he was with grabbing her purse and running out the door.

"The bitch," said Chris.

All the men at the bar looked like Gilbert Roland and were drinking rye and soda or just rye. All the women at the bar looked like Ava Gardner and were drinking Cuba Libres with twists of lemon.

"Hermano," said Franz, feeling Spanish, or Mexican, or Cuban, though there is a great difference, but Latin, "I like this place. It's what I like about the west coast of Florida, the feeling here."

His brother grimaced as he drank his beer.

The drunk at the table in front of them got up and wiped off his face and tie with a napkin. He left some money on the table and stumbled out.

"Wallace Beery in *The Champ*," said Franz.

"What?" said Chris.

"That guy."

"You're crazy," he said.

They ate their crab and walked outside. There was a strong fish wind coming in off the water. It made Franz shiver in his shirt sleeves but it felt good and he waited until Chris started the car up before he got in.

Night in the tropics was supposed to be peaceful. Buzzing insects maybe but cooler and calmer without the white heat and hiss of the day.

Franz was nervous but hoped he looked calm. He was at the old dock where the famous novelist and short story writer had once boxed the famous poet at the insistence of the poet and badly beaten him. They had boxed in the evening and the poet, wearing dark glasses and a hat, had left Port Tropique early the next morning.

The famous poet had been several years older than the famous novelist. Both of them had gone on to write about the place but neither had ever referred publicly to the boxing match, this being much to the credit of the novelist, who was not widely known for his humility. After the poet's death there was delivered to the by that time absurdly famous novelist and short story writer a letter from the poet thanking him for this kindness.

It was only a short time before his own death that the novelist admitted the incident to a reporter from a national publication with the comment that he had taken it easy on the "old man," that he could have "taken him apart" if he'd wanted to, but he'd known it would have "buried" him—the novelist—"even deeper" with the critics. A poet wasn't supposed to know how to fight, anyhow, he said, and the "old fellow" had been no exception.

Franz felt cold and uncomfortable waiting on the pier. He was on time and then he saw the running lights of the small boat coming in. He caught the line and looped it around a cleat. El Serpiente jumped onto the dock and took the suitcase. His face was yellow, one eye glowed red and the other gold. The snake handed the suitcase to a man on the boat whose face Franz could not see and the man went below with it.

There were not many stars out but Franz watched the few there were disappear and reappear. In a few minutes the man whose face he couldn't see came back out

17

and handed the suitcase back to the serpent who gave it to Franz. It was filled now so it was heavy and the snake looked quickly at Franz and without a warning remark told him to be back with it at this place at ten o'clock the next night. He jumped into the boat and Franz threw him the line and the boat moved slowly away.

Franz began immediately back to Calle Cincuenta Ocho. The gun in his left pants pocket was glued by sweat to his leg. He felt like a schoolboy embarrassed by a sudden erection while standing in front of the class, and he closed his hand around it as he walked.

There was a quarter of a million in mixed currency. Twice a week meant more than two mill a month. He looked at the cash then closed the suitcase and put it in the closet. He had made sure to have enough food and bottled water to last him at least two days, so he wouldn't have to go out.

Franz sat on the edge of the bed. No uppers. That was all right, he could make it without any. They'd better not cross him when he delivered. He'd bring the gun but there would be more than one. Two or three for sure. They needed him. Who else could they use down here? It would go smoothly and he would have twenty-five hundred. Then another next week and for however long it would go.

His penis was hard but he didn't want to masturbate. He drank some gaseosa water and belched. He wouldn't want to eat, either. He had always to have something to look forward to, for some reason that used to upset Marie. If he could find her maybe she would talk with him now about the boy. They could go to California. His cock went soft as soon as he thought about Marie. He'd pull through without her.

Marie had refused to see him and he had decided to leave New Orleans and go to California. He was walking along Esplanade when a big gold several-year-old Buick pulled up to the curb and a bearded guy with a black silk headband leaned out the window and asked in a Georgia drawl if he knew where there might be a place to stay for the night. Franz saw there were two girls with him in the car. They talked for a few minutes, and Franz invited him and the girls up to his friend Roget's apartment, where he was headed, around the corner.

Jay was just out of the Marines. He'd picked up the girls in New York, where he'd been discharged, driven them first to Macon, where he stopped to see his mother, then to New Orleans, where he hoped to find work. The girls were runaways, both sixteen, one blonde and cute with a fabulous figure, the other not so cute but talkative. The blonde didn't talk much, her name was Stoney. Jay seemed attached to the brunette, Natalie.

Jay told a story about being gas-attacked in Nam while watching a movie camped out in the field. He'd been sitting in a lawn chair smoking reefer and by the time he folded up the chair and made it to the tent to get his gas mask the attack was over. He was so stoned he'd never have even noticed they were being attacked unless somebody had screamed at him. It hadn't mattered anyway, he said, he just took the lawn chair back to where he'd been sitting before the raid, unfolded it, sat down and lit up another joint. He'd been wounded three times, he said, his stomach was all rearranged, nothing went where it should, so he'd been given a medical discharge.

Roget was frightened of Jay, but liked Natalie, so he invited them to stay. Franz slept with Stoney that night. Her body was perfectly smooth, she let him manipulate her to his satisfaction and he had successfully fought off

20

any incapacitating thought of Marie. Franz did not want to have to think about anything or talk seriously, and Stoney made no demands, rarely spoke, and Franz wound up taking her with him to California.

Stoney looked at least twenty, with that exquisite body nobody would believe she was only sixteen, and she was good company on the long ride. Jay, Roget later wrote Franz, went back to Georgia, and Natalie stayed in New Orleans for awhile before returning to New York. She slept in her blue jeans, Roget said, and wouldn't do anything but jack him off.

That certainly wasn't the case with Stoney. She and Franz screwed their way across the continent, taking their time. It was a very cold winter with hazardous driving much of the way. They often stopped at motels at three in the afternoon, made love, napped for awhile, then got up to check out whatever town they were in. Stoney was a big hit at truck stops. She had a wide mouth, large blue heavy-lidded eyes, a fresh creamy complexion, and those big breasts. The truckers ate it up, politely offered her rides, winked at Franz. He got a kick out of it and joked with them, but Stoney was embarrassed and wouldn't say anything, just grinned and sipped her coke, covering her face with one hand. She was a shy kid, she didn't know how to handle herself, and Franz took care of her the best he could.

He liked her but had no intention of pursuing their relationship after they got to California. She knew this, acknowledged it, and Franz paid their way west. Once they arrived in San Francisco, however, Stoney told him that she wanted to stay with him, and Franz said all right, but only until she found a job and had a little money so that she could operate on her own.

It turned out to be several weeks before Stoney moved into her own place. She worked as a carhop at a drive-in, and Franz saw her only occasionally after that. She would show up at two in the morning, after her shift ended, and stay with him. However, after she had arrived a couple of times and found him with other women, she stopped coming around. Franz hoped she was all right, and was concerned enough to call her every so often to find out how she was doing.

One night Franz phoned and a girl told him that Stoney had gone to live in Los Angeles. She had left the week before and hadn't left any forwarding address. It wasn't until almost a year later that Franz heard from her. She wrote that she was living in Hollywood, working as a model, doing well, she had plenty of money and to please visit her if ever he happened to be down that way.

It so happened that a few weeks later Franz was in LA and called Stoney. She was glad to hear from him and told him to come right over. She answered the door wearing a floor-length green nightgown, a feather boa wrapped around her neck. Her eyes were so heavily made up that it was difficult to tell what color they were, and she had dyed her hair red and grown it long. Worst of all, she was fat, her beautiful body had lost its natural lines. Her bosom was grotesquely large and flabby looking, spilling out of the flimsy gown. She was smoking a black cigarette in a tarnished gold-plated holder.

Stoney was living with a girl named Mona in a small run-down cottage close to Hollywood Boulevard. When Franz arrived, Mona was sitting on a moth-eaten divan smoking dope with two emaciated young men. Stoney introduced Franz to them, they barely nodded, and Stoney took him by the hand to her room in the rear of the house.

She told Franz how thankful she was that he had taken her with him to California, how wonderful everything was, and she kissed him. She unzipped his pants and took out his cock, rubbed it between her enormous breasts, then sucked him off sloppily and loudly, smearing her overly-applied orange lipstick over her cheeks and chin. Franz lay back on the bed, closed his eyes and let her make him come. When he looked up at her she was smiling, wiping her face with the edge of the bedspread.

"Would you like to see some of my pictures?" she asked.

When Franz said all right she brought out a stack of magazines and handed them to him. She sat next to him on the bed and pointed out what she thought were the best shots.

They were hardcore sex books with photographs of Stoney in every position imaginable that still allowed a good view of her crotch: bending backwards, forwards, straddling. There were top-hat-and-cane numbers, a classic dangling cigarette pose, and one of her being licked by a German shepherd, but most of them were up-front closeups with Stoney clad only in a garter belt. She was proud of them. A producer had promised her a part in a movie. Once she was in the movies she wouldn't have to do this kind of thing anymore.

"I'm doing okay, don't you think?" she asked.

When Franz didn't answer she said, "Please don't worry about me. Really, I know what I'm doing." She lit a black cigarette. "You know," she told him, "I'm seventeen now. Everyone down here thinks I'm twenty-two. I'll be all right, and besides, I've got lots of time."

Franz made himself tea and looked across the crumbling yellow rooftops at the unmoving palms. Before he'd come to Port Tropique Franz hadn't known that "Latin" was a dirty word, that it was, to quote Carpentier, as good as saying rabble, small fry, or negro rebels. Language, he decided, was possibly the most emotionally confusing issue in the world, the supreme cause of revolution and assassination.

It was night and the trees did not move. A bad sign, Franz thought, and he gave some whisky to the tea. He drank some and sweated. He drank some more and sweated and waited and tried to stop himself from dreaming of what had already taken place and what he could no longer control. There was little point to life, he felt, if there was no controlling at least some small part of it.

He kept expecting to see Marlene Dietrich looking like she did as the fortune-telling bordertown café hostess in *Touch of Evil* come walking slowly down Calle Cincuenta Ocho. It was the proper street for it and tonight was the right night. What did she say at the end after Orson Welles got popped? He was a great detective but he was a lousy cop. Something like that.

Franz cracked the second bottle of Irish. It's tough for anyone who's awake at this hour, he thought, no matter what they think they have to look forward to.

Marie was not to blame. Not her, nor himself. Why she made him sweat still he could not explain unless it was because of the boy. It might well be he truly owed her for that, or possibly she owed him, but it shouldn't make him sweat like he did.

He had to admit he would like to have her with him now. Not here but over in the Tropique where they would have their own bathroom, and he could watch her undress, step out of her little pants with her breasts half out of the slip, and have them both be twenty years old and harmless to all but themselves.

He sat up quickly when he heard the shots. There were three fast pops and he waited until thirty seconds had gone by before looking out the window but he could see nothing. If this were the States it might be kids killing lizards but here kids didn't have guns and those who did employed them diplomatically by shooting diplomats.

It suddenly occurred to Franz that yesterday had been his fortieth birthday.

He had seen a wonderful photograph of Max Kroner once in an old *Life* magazine in a barber shop. Franz had been about nine or ten years old at the time and had wondered why he had to take a haircut when this old guy standing on a log in a forest with a rifle slung over one arm and a machete in his belt had white hair hanging to his shoulders.

"That's because he lives in a jungle, dear," said his mother.

There were three porters in baggy pants with machetes in their belts and huaraches and wide-brimmed hats holding rifles and gunny sacks standing on the log behind Max Kroner in the photograph. The caption underneath said that Kroner was a pioneer in the study of ancient Indian civilizations, one of the last of the oldtime adventurers. Behind the men on the log, the young Franz knew, were the jaguars and snakes and cannibals.

Compared to his companions Max Kroner was tall and thin, his skeletal, Nordic face was very handsome, and he looked, to quote a favorite expression of Franz's mother's, trés content.

The rebels were in Domingo City. At least that's what the waiters were saying in The Habana. If it was true that meant the governor would be at his villa outside of Port Tropique and there would be more soldiers in and around the town. A genuine fear would mean the soldiers stopping gringos to search them and check their papers. He hoped it wasn't going to be that bad.

He heard several more shots during the night but managed to get some sleep anyway.

Franz was at the old dock at nine fifty-five. At exactly ten o'clock he heard the boat engine. The boat ran dark up next to the pier and idled and someone shone a blinding light in his face.

"Put down the suitcase and walk away twenty paces," a man shouted.

They kept the light in his eyes and from twenty paces he could see nothing. It seemed to take a long time and Franz got worried. He wanted to say something about his being paid but he did not. Instead he stood and fidgeted and fingered the .32 in his right coat pocket and the .38 in his left. It was too hot even at this time of night to be wearing a jacket but he had promised himself to go down wailing if it came to it and he had no other way to pack the iron.

Suddenly the dock went dark again and the boat was moving out. Franz walked quickly back to where he'd left the suitcase. It was lying open and there was money in it. He lit a match and counted it. There was twenty-five hundred on the nose. He stuffed the cash into his pockets and put the guns into the suitcase, locked it up and started walking. He'd passed a few soldiers on the way out but there didn't appear to be anything out of the ordinary. God bless the governor, thought Franz. God bless him a little longer, then perhaps both he and I will get away with our heads and something extra.

Franz's first practical awareness of business occurred on his fifteenth birthday when a black man blew Benjamin Finestone's face off with a shotgun. Finestone owned a Cadillac agency in Gretna and lived in a mansion on St. Charles Avenue. Willis Jones, the man who killed him, had bought a Cadillac from Finestone Motors for fifty dollars down and however much a month and by the time the matter got out of hand for good he'd paid almost twice over the price of the model he'd purchased and still owed a thousand dollars.

That particular Coup de Ville had long since ceased to exist as a functional item but according to the terms of the sale as defined in the Finestone Motors contract that was immaterial. All that mattered was that the customer still owed interest on the payments. A deal is a deal, Benjamin Finestone had said before Willis Jones removed his eyes, nose, mouth and chin.

Willis had been greatly disturbed by the collection agency hounding him at the car wash and bothering his wife at home. He couldn't get out from under the debt, he said, and called Benjamin Finestone a real Jew, which made Finestone angry. Finestone called Willis a jungle bunny and told him to get out of his office. There was more yelling and then the terrific noise which made the agency salesmen throw themselves under cars on the showroom floor.

Willis Jones was sitting in a chair in Benjamin Finestone's office when the cops arrived. The shotgun was on the floor and he did not give them any trouble.

Smokey Robinson singing "Bad Girl" kept going through his head. A Mohawk high steel worker he'd once been on a job with named Luther Two Ax had liked that song and used to repeat the first line of it over and over: "She's not a bad girl because/she made me see/ how love could be."

Franz wandered around town that day feeling the new money in his pocket. He stopped twice to drink papaya milkshakes. He already had the runs so it didn't matter what he ate or drank, he had been fairly cavalier about it anyway, and he stood with a papaya drink in his hand humming "Bad Girl" and watching the army troops filter into the city.

So it was true about the battle at Ciudad Domingo. These soldiers looked tired and shabby and la gente spoke muy rápido today, which, unlike their Caribbean cousins, was uncharacteristic.

He gave two pesos to the thing folded up like a crushed spider outside The Habana and sat down at a table close to the street. An Indian boy came in and sat in the chair opposite him at the table and asked if he wanted to buy a flower, holding up a thin-stemmed red paper rose. Franz gave him fifty centavos and the boy ran off without giving him anything.

The waiter with the most gold teeth of any of the waiters in the café and whose station included those tables nearest the street where the tourists were encouraged to sit said that the governor was rumoured to be about to depart the country on a diplomatic mission to an unnamed destination. So far as he, the head waiter, could discern, the imminence of the governor's journey, and quite possibly the duration of his absence, was dependent largely on the results of the al fresco political conference currently being concluded in Domingo.

Franz ordered a dish of guava con queso and an espresso and watched the traffic crawl. The headwaiter's

English was very good. If the situation in Port Tropique became really impossible he would have no difficulty getting a job in Miami or New York.

Things were heating up in the Montejo district. All along the Calle Montejo people were carrying furniture down the stairs of the big houses and loading it into trucks and cars. Well-dressed old ladies clutching elaborately carved and decorated boxes were being assisted down the stairs and into vehicles.

Franz walked up and down the streets of the Section Montejo watching the rich folks panic. He spent the rest of the afternoon this way and an hour or so after it had become dark he stopped at the Café Biarritz for a beer.

He sat at a sidewalk table in order to better observe the continuing exodus and had half finished his beer when the same Indian boy who had approached him earlier in the day at The Habana came up to him and asked him if he wanted to buy a flower. Franz told the boy he had paid him fifty centavos that afternoon for a flower and that he had gone off without giving him one.

The boy, who could not have been more than seven or eight years old, acting in the fashion of the Indians of that region, did not look at Franz but stood absolutely still staring at the cars stream by, then suddenly put on the table the same artificial rose he had offered Franz at The Habana and walked swiftly away.

He and Marie had once spent a night in El Paso, a maddening, sprawling industrial town of perpetual flashing lights, sirens, and speeding cars and trucks. Franz still could not dismiss from his mind the sight of an overturned Buick in front of a Mexican nightclub, the passengers trapped inside while people stood around on the sidewalk and in the street laughing and drinking, music blaring, waiting for the cops to arrive.

There was a similar kind of chaotic, unsettled feeling tonight in Port Tropique. The zócalo was unusually crowded, and the sky was perfectly clear with a soft breeze coming in off the Gulf which made the salt air so balmy that Franz wanted to sit out in it all night. Young children ran and played around the fountain. Lovers sat on the benches holding hands and whispering. Men stood around in small groups arguing and telling stories and smoking. Women sat and nursed their babies and talked and laughed among themselves. It was almost midnight of a mid-week day and there was a holiday atmosphere as if it were festival time.

Franz bit off the end of one of the four six peso Cuban cigars he had bought at the Biarritz, tongued and lit it and sat on a bench in the square waiting and wondering like everyone else who had nothing much to lose.

The Junkanoo Kings, a black rhumba band from Key West, were performing in the bar of the Hotel Consuelo del Carmen where Renaldo and his big ugly bear of a partner met Franz. The bear kept his eyes on the band and El Serpiente did the talking.

The next shipment was being hurried through due to the unpredictable nature of current events. Franz was to be at the dock the next night by eleven and return at the same hour of the following day. There would be another transfer as soon as possible thereafter. Raoul de Avila, the commander of the rebel forces, the serpent confided, would be a more difficult fellow to deal with than the present governor.

"Like all revolutionary leaders," said Renaldo, "he calls himself a communist or a socialist or a republican but he is only a bandit like the rest of us poor boys. But let us not worry too much. There are even in the best of times uncertainties."

After the serpent and the bear had departed, Franz ordered a Cuba Libre and silently saluted the memory of Errol Flynn.

Twelve years ago, Franz thought, his mother still had her looks and was half-owner of a three-storey house in the Garden District of New Orleans. She was forty-eight years old, drove a nice car, had a respectable, secure job as a receptionist at a private hospital, and only herself and Franz's thirteen-year-old sister to support.

Then she had married again and moved to Houston, sold her interest in the house for less than she should have, and settled down to become a housewife, confident that her husband would be an able provider for her and her daughter. Now she was sixty, her looks much diminished due to her being greatly overweight, a condition brought on by nervousness, had no money in the bank to speak of, living in an apartment on a major thoroughfare, without a job, her husband desperately struggling to salvage some capital from his defunct business operations. Franz's sister was living in Atlanta, trying to work her way through college. All his mother really had were her two old cats, her only dependable companions.

Once a beautiful, fairly well-to-do woman, his mother was greatly disappointed, disillusioned and saddened by the turn her life had taken. By this time she felt she would be living out a comfortable matronage. However, her spirits were often still high, and she was able to take some solace in the little she did have. There were certainly worse stories than hers, but being in advanced middle age, with no money or real prospects, especially after having had more than enough of both at various times, and having abandoned all faith in her husband, was a far from satisfactory condition that contributed little toward Franz's peace of mind.

The second pick-up went as smoothly as the first. Franz looked in the suitcase, saw there was about the same amount in similar denominations, closed it up and stuck it away.

He considered leaving it and going down to The Habana or the hotel for a drink but decided he'd better stay put just in case. No sense in getting careless at this point. Besides, what would he do if the cash got ripped? He'd never be able to cover it, and both sides would be sure he had conspired with the other and as the saying goes if one didn't get him the other would. No, he'd stick it out until tomorrow night. It was extremely doubtful that he would ever again have a quarter of a million dollars in clean, easily passable bills in his possession even for twenty-four hours. Not unless he stuck up a bank. He wasn't going to inherit anything, that was certain.

The thought of keeping it, of just taking the suitcase and getting on a plane, occurred to him, but the idea of running for the rest of his assuredly short life scotched its appeal. He would take it easy, collect what he could for as long as the scam held, and go away happy, or, if not necessarily happy, on at least reasonable terms with his shadow.

Raoul de Avila was hardly a poor boy. He came from an upper-middle-class Spanish family whose emigration had been accomplished within the last generation. Their fortune was made in the lace business and the young Raoul was given the benefit of a Catholic education plus private tutelage in English and French.

Raoul was sent to the Universidad de Barcelona where he took an undergraduate degree in philosophy and a graduate degree in advanced Russian. Next was Yale, where he took an M.A. in anthropology, and then the Universidad de Ciudad Domingo, where he earned a doctorate in political science in the same year that his parents once again took up permanent residence in Spain.

The young doctor of political thought spent the following few years traveling and working in Central and South America and Cuba. Upon his return to his native country Raoul, now sporting Fidel-like whiskers and spouting a like rhetoric, swiftly incurred the wrath of the authorities by moving from province to province, accompanied by a phalanx of supporters, speaking out at every opportunity against the injustices wrought upon the peons by the ruling class and entreating citizens everywhere to rise up as one and knock the fat cat off their collective backs.

Raoul and his band were declared to be enemies of the state, a designation they welcomed, and were soon headquartered at a peripatetic jungle camp from which they initiated raids on provincial armories, slowly gathering strength in numbers as well as weapons.

VIVA RAOUL! posters appeared in the villages, towns and cities throughout the country. It was rumoured that funds were being collected on the campuses of colleges and universities in the United States to aid Raoul de Avila's guerrillas but if so these contributions were never received by the revolutionary forces.

Rifles and money were supposedly being smuggled to them by emissaries of China, Cuba and the Soviet Union, and at one point Raoul was alleged to be in Moscow on a support-gathering mission, but these reports remained unconfirmed.

When interviewed in Barcelona about the activities of his son Raoul's father told the world press that he did not personally intend to continue working forever, and that upon his retirement he expected Raoul to assume the supervision of the family's lace business.

Now that Ciudad Domingo's capitulation was a fore-gone conclusion, the reporters and photographers began to descend on Port Tropique. Franz was sitting in The Habana discussing with Alfonso the head waiter the various avenues of escape open to the governor and his entourage when a tall, fair-haired man wearing wire-rim dark glasses and a sweat-stained bush shirt sat down opposite him and asked if Franz minded his sharing the table. Franz looked around the café and noted that there were only a few scattered customers in the place and many empty tables before saying he did not.

"Do you live in Port Tropique?" the man asked him.

"Do you wish to order, señor?" said Alfonso.

"Oh, yeah, bring me a Coke."

"Si, señor. Es todo?"

"Yes. And a slice of lemon."

Alfonso left and the man returned his attention to Franz.

"Do you?"

"For now."

"Been here long?"

"A while. You're a journalist."

"Washington Post. Paul Nathan."

"Come from Domingo?"

The journalist snorted. "That pit. Nothing but blood and shit, the almighty stench of death. John Reed would have loved it."

"You don't find the revolution fascinating?" Franz asked.

"All these serápetistas ever do is play a game of grue-some musical chairs. You can't tell the dictators without a scorecard, you know. Africa's where it's really going down in a big way. Zambia, Rhodesia, Mozambique. Bitch of a scene there, I tell you. Bastards here cut a few throats, burn down a church and figure it's all over."

"How about Raoul? Did you get to talk with him?"

"El Jefe refuses to speak anything but Spanish now, the peasant dialect yet. Half his advisers work for the CIA and he's got the balls to call himself a liberator."

The reporter drank his Coke straight down and sucked on the lemon.

"What's your name?"

"Hall."

"Yank?"

Franz nodded. "Yes and no. I grew up in New Orleans."

"What are you doing here?"

"Writing a book about Benjamin Franklin."

Nathan snickered. "Pretty strange place to pick for that, isn't it?"

"I don't know. Gore Vidal wrote *Burr* in Rome. Robert Graves wrote *I, Claudius* in Mallorca. Mary Renault wrote *The Persian Boy* in Cape Town. Sometimes the proper perspective is more easily attained from a distance."

Nathan took off his dark glasses. His eyes were a practically-colorless blue. Franz guessed he was about thirty-five years old.

"Written many books?" the journalist asked.

"No," said Franz, "this is the first one."

Nathan put his glasses back on and stood up.

"Well, I've got to find a place to clean up and kip. Any suggestions?"

"The Tropique, next door, is the closest thing to The Plaza, but if you want a good drink you have to go to The Consuelo, across the square."

"I'll try next door. Good luck. I hope the shooting match won't interfere with your work."

"Thanks," said Franz. "So do I."

After the reporter had gone Alfonso came over and picked up his glass and the two pesos he'd left on the table.

"Tell me, Alfonso," Franz said, "what will you do if this Raoul turns out really to be a communist?"

Alfonso considered the question for a moment, then showed many of his gold teeth.

"I think then I will get married, señor, and manufacture a great number of comrades for the cause."

Franz had a bit in excess of five thousand dollars now, the second drop having gone off without a hitch. This time the party had been less concerned about exposure and had openly conducted the transfer. Two Chinese had effected the exchange while a white man wearing a black and gold dime store captain's hat and a yellow terrycloth shirt watched from the boat.

Franz had waited until the Chinese had gone back aboard before picking up his money. As he was folding it into his pockets the man in the captain's hat and terrycloth shirt shouted, "Viva Raoul!" and laughed sarcastically as the boat pulled away.

Franz fastened the suitcase and stood on the dock watching them go. "Viva la Franz!" he said.

The governor held a press conference in the Presidential Suite of the Hotel Tropique. Unlike Batista at his New Year's Eve party where he announced his immediate departure due to the advance of the rebels on Havana, the governor of Port Tropique told the dozen or so representatives of the international wire services, foreign bureaus of great newspapers, free-lance journalists, photographers, and the two or three employees of the hotel who were handing out free drinks, that the insurgents were being repelled at the eastern frontier of Ciudad Domingo and those few who remained following their decimation by the Nacionalistas would soon be, as the Norte Americanos say, making little ones out of big ones. The governor smiled very widely when he said this, and then expressed his sincerest desire that those diligent individuals who had traveled so far to report the truth of the situation to the rest of the world should enjoy their stay in his paradise of a country and return to their own with the most favorable of impressions.

Following the conclusion of his remarks the governor, still smiling widely, refused politely to answer any questions and, escorted by a quartet of heavily armed bodyguards, got into his cream-colored Mercedes-Benz limousine with the bullet-proofed windows and was driven without delay to the airport where he boarded a jet which was the property of an international oil cartel and was flown to London, where his wife and children had gone several days before on a shopping trip.

Waiting for Renaldo in the bar of the Hotel Consuelo del Carmen Franz was approached by two young Japanese men, one of whom inquired in very precise English whether or not he was familiar with the work of the American jazz musician Stan Getz.

"Yes," said Franz.

"You know 'Smaw Hoteru'?"

" 'My Ode Frame,' " said the second of the Japanese men.

"What do you think of Bossa Nova?" asked the first Japanese.

"I am mad with joy over it," said the second Japanese.

"Very good, very good," said the first Japanese. "This is a very good time, do you not agree?"

"Sure," said Franz.

"Do you do your hanging around in this place?" asked the first one.

"Sometimes. Would you like a drink?"

"Beefeaters," said the second Japanese.

"Very much, yes," said the first.

Franz ordered the drinks and asked them what they were doing in Port Tropique.

"We are in the selling of industrial equipment," said the first Japanese. "For the weaving of cloth."

"And you like American jazz?"

"Hai, hai," said the second one. "Very much so."

"We miss very much jazz where we are living in Domingo City," said the first.

Franz spotted Renaldo alone at a table.

"Please excuse me gentlemen," he said, "but I must speak with someone."

"Of course," said the first Japanese, "it is our pleasure."

El Serpiente asked Franz who the two Orientals at the bar were.

"Fans of Stan Getz," he said. "They're everywhere."

The next rendez-vous, Renaldo had told Franz, would not be for another week, and that, of course, would depend on the prevailing political situation.

When Franz first came to Port Tropique he inquired about the whorehouses and was told they had been closed down by the governor when he had taken office two years before. Since then Franz had learned of a place in Uxpan, a little town a few miles in the direction of Ciudad Domingo, and after his chat with the serpent he hired one of the taxis parked around the zócalo to take him there.

He told the taxi to wait. Inside he found a fat woman he took to be the madam and two thin Indian girls in lace dresses who, he guessed, were about fourteen years old. They were sitting next to each other on kitchen chairs holding hands. Neither of them wore shoes or underwear. Franz chose the one with the clearest complexion, paid the madam, and followed the girl to another room.

There was a terrific stink coming from the goat pen and chicken shack next to the house so Franz got it over with quickly.

As he was getting into the taxi a finely profiled white-haired woman in a red 1949 Buick Roadmaster convertible drove past, heading toward Domingo.

"Do you know who that woman was?" Franz asked the driver.

"Señora Kroner," he said. "A fine lady. She has lived here many years. We return now to Port Tropique?"

"What do you think of the rebels?" asked Franz. "Will they win?"

The driver shrugged. "Quien sabes, señor? Who knows what side God is on?"

"The communists don't believe in God."

"Perhaps," said the driver. "But what matters is if God believes in them. We return now?"

"Now."

46

In his sleep Franz saw Marie as he had seen her that first time in his mother's house on St. Charles. She was with her parents, having just returned from a trip to Europe following her graduation from Sophie Newcomb.

Sitting up like a lioness' proud head reared, a wide-eyed, dangerous, saber-bright beauty, Marie was browned and blond from the Italian sun, her slim long legs folded delicately under a thin yellow cotton dress, blond strands fallen over almond eyes, nose slightly crooked, tilted gently away from lips full and moist in a natural pout. It was like seeing Ingrid Bergman at twenty waiting at a bus stop.

Then they were on the deck of the ferry about to dock at Otaru, passing the Krûng Siam, a battered, rusty tub of a freighter, tiny, about six hundred tons, out of Bangkok. There was snow on the mountains and the sky was overcast, semi-rainy and bone-cold like late winter Oregon coastal towns. The wooden buildings reminded Franz even more of the Pacific Northwest, there was early morning smoke in the air, and he felt comfortable. It was Marie's birthday, they were on their honeymoon, on their way to Sapporo in northern Japan. Franz reached over for her hand and then awoke, covered with sweat, holding the gun.

How's the book coming?" It was Nathan, the man from the *Washington Post*.

"Oh, hello. All right, thanks."

Franz took his change off the magnet the taco vendor used to handle coins, put them in his pocket, and bit into his taco.

"Have a beer?" asked Nathan.

Franz nodded, and they went across the street to the Angel Negro. They took a table in the rear, as far from the jukebox as possible. The reporter ordered four Dos Equis but they didn't have Dos Equis so he ordered four Montezumas. The waiter apologized for not having that brand either and Franz told him to bring Superiors and the waiter thanked him and went off to get them.

"I'm surprised to see you're still here," said Franz. "I thought by now you would have found a more interesting conflict to engage your reportorial talents."

"You talk like a writer. Are you sure this is your first book you're working on?"

"Positive."

The waiter set down the four beers and four glasses.

"We'll only need two," Nathan said.

The waiter grinned and nodded and walked away, leaving the four glasses.

Franz swallowed the last of his taco and washed it down with a swig of Superior.

"No," said Nathan, "after the governor skipped I figured I'd better stick around and see what happened." He laughed.

"What's so funny?"

"Did you ever see the governor?"

"Not in the flesh, why?"

"I was at that farce of a press conference at The Tropique, and without the mustache he could have doubled for Peter Lorre in *The Maltese falcon*."

"Joel Cairo," said Franz.

"What?"

"That was his name in the picture, Joel Cairo."

"This place is a good setting for a movie. All it needs is Hoagy Carmichael instead of the jukebox."

"The music would certainly be better. They made *Treasure of the Sierra Madre* around here. Did you ever read any of B. Traven's books?"

"No, who was he?"

"A German who lived here for forty years, most of it in the bush."

"Like Maximilian Kroner."

"Sort of. You know about Kroner then?"

"Only what was in the papers when he died. I found out his widow's still alive. She lives out by Uxpan. I thought while I was waiting for Raoul and his merry men to storm the citadel it might be worth a trip out there. Do an interview with the wife of a legend, that sort of thing. Want to come along? I've rented a car."

"Why not," said Franz. "A writer always welcomes an excuse not to write."

Franz didn't say anything when they passed the house with the Indian girls. The chickens were walking in and out of the doorway and he wondered if he had the clap. It would be the end of the week before he knew for sure.

Frau Kroner's finca was named "Bom Retiro," Portuguese for Good Retreat. She had grown up in Lisbon, where her father had been the German ambassador. She'd met Max Kroner in Cuernavaca, at an archaeological conference where they had both presented papers. They fell in love almost immediately and were married a month later in Acapulco.

Her family were not pleased with the marriage and severed all but the most formal of relations with her. Despite the fact that her new husband was then still a professor at Harvard, it was not their idea of a proper match, having expected that she would eventually marry someone in the diplomatic service. But Hilda Baumann was an independent young woman. She had defied her parents before, by studying anthropology and archaeology instead of pursuing the musical career they had intended for her.

When it became clear that her marriage to Kroner was not going to be an impetuous, short-lived affair, they cut her off entirely from the family inheritance. Even after Max's dismissal from the faculty at Harvard for alcoholism and his and Hilda's difficult next few years, her family would not be moved, instead expecting that this would finally bring her to her senses and that she would leave him.

But it was not to be. The Kroners recovered and found their spiritual as well as physical home in the jungle. With the help of local Indians they built what Hilda christened Bom Retiro, and she had remained there ever since. After Max's death her mother, who was still alive but an invalid in Munich, at last wrote and asked Hilda to come live with her, but she refused. Shortly thereafter her mother had died and, despite the years of estrangement, left the family fortune to Hilda, which insured her a lifetime free from monetary worries. Hilda used the money not only for herself but to improve the living conditions of the Indians of the surrounding area, and had become something of a legend in her own right.

Nathan drove too fast for the narrow highway, and Franz kept expecting him to run down a peasant with a load of wood on his back around every bend, but no such calamity occurred, and soon they were pulling up the white-stoned entry road to Bom Retiro.

She's supposed to be a pretty sharp old gal," said Nathan. A guy from UPI at the hotel said she apparently used to be quite a beauty."

Frau Kroner was at home. Franz noticed her red Buick convertible parked at the side of the house. A pair of Bantam roosters strutted back and forth in front of it like legation guards, stopping to peck at pebbles ensconced in the treads of the tires.

Franz and Nathan were admitted by an old Indian woman and asked to please wait in the front room. The walls were decorated with colorful weavings and pictures of the Kroners at the sites of ancient temples. The photograph of Max Kroner and three companions standing on a log in a swamp that Franz had seen in *Life* magazine when he was a boy was there, as well as one of the anthropology department faculty at Harvard before the war, in which Kroner cut by far the most outstanding figure, standing slightly apart from his fellow professors, his Barrymore-like profile directed away from the others as if responding to a call only he could hear.

Hilda Kroner, despite her snow-white hair, looked like a woman of no more than fifty-five, though she had to be at least seventy. She wore an orange lace blouse and swirling black skirt embroidered in green and orange with the figures of serpents. Franz immediately thought of Ava Gardner dancing in the moonlight on the Mexican beach with her two servant boys in *Night of the Iguana*.

They introduced themselves, apologized for not having made an appointment, their coming having been a spur-of-the-moment decision, and Paul Nathan said that he would be honored if she could spare them a few moments to talk about her life with Max Kroner and what she had been doing since his death. Frau Kroner averred as to how the former would take quite a bit longer to accomplish than a few moments, but if they

52

would follow her out to the terrace close on the garden she would be glad to provide them with a fruit drink and a short chat.

When they were seated she explained that alcohol of any kind had always been forbidden at Bom Retiro. The Indian woman who had let Franz and Nathan in then served each of them a glass of coconut milk.

"Now," said Hilda Kroner, "what would you like to know about Max and me that has not already been written?"

It surprised Franz that she spoke American English without the least trace of an accent of any kind. In response to Nathan's questions she talked for a while about how dedicated a man Max had been, and how the Indians had considered him a real compañero and respected him for his ability to operate with equal facility in so many different cultures. She then detailed briefly her own recent efforts at attempting to properly integrate the modern and traditional in that particular region.

Nathan asked what she thought of the rebellion and what changes could likely be expected in the event Raoul de Avila seized control of the government.

"He will win, I am certain," she said. "Like Max, he speaks to the people as equals. What will happen once he assumes responsibility for them is another question. A socialist government of the type Raoul is likely to establish will be especially vulnerable to outside interference.

"When Max helped to organize the Uxtil land reform movement I was afraid he would be murdered, and he undoubtedly would have been had not the workers stayed by him the entire time. No, it will be difficult for Raoul to survive personally, let alone politically. I only hope he has a little time to help begin the process of education the people so desperately need in order to assert themselves and take possession of what is rightfully theirs."

Frau Kroner spoke to them a bit more and then said she had work to do, that it had been a pleasure to have met them. She shook their hands firmly and excused herself, leaving the Indian woman to escort them to the door.

When Nathan and Franz drove back through Uxpan the two Indian prostitutes were in front of the house playing catch.

Franz's father had died in a hospital, the most igno-minious of places in which to die. Nobody wants to die in a hospital. Who wouldn't rather be run through in a duel on a Caribbean beach like Basil Rathbone in *Captain Blood* and have the waves spill over their bloody curls? Or even be murdered in bed by an intruder? Any place but in a soulless, antiseptic, public convenience.

A revolution wouldn't be so bad to go out in, Franz thought. To be caught in the street between sides and get cut down by cross-fire during a valiant attempt to carry an old woman to safety, something like that. But death was rarely so romantically accommodating. Usually they carried you out of the house on Sunday and you never came back for Monday.

After Max Kroner died, his widow said, the Indians burned his body, deposited most of his ashes in a silver urn which was kept at Bom Retiro, and scattered the rest to the four winds from atop a pyramid deep in the jungle. At least that meant something to the Indians.

"Can you believe it?" Paul Nathan said to Franz the next morning in The Habana. "The governor had a heart attack in London. He's dead, they're flying his body back here to be buried."

"Did he die in a hospital?" asked Franz.

"No, at some royal do. He was dancing with a Rumanian princess and collapsed in her arms."

"The lucky stiff," Franz said.

The rain began during the night. It woke Franz and he went over to the window, lit up the next to the last of the six peso Cubanos, and sat and looked out at it. The initial cloudburst had filled the street instantly and now it settled into a steady downpour. This was the real beginning of the rainy season. Everyone had been saying it was late this year.

He didn't know whether this would aid the rebels or make it more difficult for them. He realized he didn't really care. Renaldo's boys would work something out with them or anyone else. They'd already tied down the new governor, Torres or Perez or whatever his name was. Raoul would get in all right, though, rain or no rain.

Marie would be a help now. The heat, the rain, the jungle, the revolution, none of it would bother her, not if she were in love with him, and she wouldn't be with him if she weren't in love with him. I guess that's why she isn't here, Franz thought, and laughed out loud.

There was a woman he'd met on a train, he couldn't remember her name, a redhead with green eyes and tobacco-stained teeth, who had spent some time in Port Tropique, she said. The train was going from Oakland to Salt Lake City, she'd been visiting friends in San Francisco and was on her way home.

She was about forty-five, a little strange in the head, Franz thought after a few minutes of conversation, but not unattractive in a floozyish way, and he'd tried to get her to stay with him that night in Salt Lake, but she wouldn't have any part of it. Not that she really might not like to, she explained, but it was because of a bad experience with another younger man she'd trusted.

It had happened when she and her now ex-husband were moving to Seattle, where she'd lived for four years before returning to Utah. Her husband had gone on ahead with most of their belongings to take a job, and she'd stayed behind to clean out the last of the stuff from the house in Salt Lake City, loading it into the car that she was driving to Seattle. Their next door neighbor, a young guy who'd lost a hand in the early stages of the Vietnam war, whom she liked, said he would help her drive, that he had always wanted to visit Seattle anyway.

She agreed, and everything went well, she told Franz, until they hit Boise. They pulled into a motel and before she could object, he'd asked for one room, not two, and taken the money from her purse to pay the clerk. She was shocked, she said, but at that point she hadn't wanted to cause a scene.

Once they were in the room she told him she had no intention of sleeping with him, and that she'd thought it was understood they would each pay their expenses separately. He turned really ugly then, she said.

"Do you think I'd be with an older woman," he shouted,"if she weren't paying my way?"

"Then he beat the *shit* out of me," she said deliberately, teeth clenched, obviously still stung by it. After a moment she told Franz that as soon as she could get away she'd run out of the motel and driven straight through to Seattle.

"What did you tell your husband?" Franz asked. "About the bruises."

"Oh," she said,"I told him I'd picked up a hitchhiker who'd tried to rob me. He believed me and that was the end of it. The creep who did it left Utah. I don't know where he went and I don't want to know. So you see how difficult it would be for me to trust you."

Franz had agreed, he understood, he said, and hadn't pushed the issue. He re-lit the Cubana Especial and puffed on it, watching the rain hammer the adobes. It had been a while since he had been tempted to trust someone himself. He couldn't decide whether that was good or bad, so he let it pass.

J ane Fury was about to leave the country. She operated an art gallery in the Hotel Tropique during the tourist season, and now that the heavy rains had begun she was closing down for the year and going to Phoenix.

Jane was coming out of the Tropique when Manuel Santos, the bookstore owner, spotted her from across the street. He ran over and insisted that she have a drink with him before she left town. Since she planned to leave the next day she told him it would have to be right then. Manuel was very glad to accommodate her every wish, as he put it, and suggested The Habana.

The café was crowded and noisy. It seemed as if everyone who was still in the city was there. Paul Nathan noticed Jane and Manuel looking around for a place to sit and went over and told them that they were welcome to share a table with him and his friend. Manuel was not eager to share with others the short time he would have with the señora and kept craning his neck around in a search for a vacant table, but there were none and Jane gratefully accepted Nathan's offer.

Jane Fury was a tall, large-boned, attractive, dark-haired, dark-eyed woman of indeterminate middle age. A former Main Line Philadelphia housewife, she had left her lawyer husband and three children five years before for a cowboy she met at a benefit rodeo for Vietnamese orphans and gone to live with him on a ranch near Gila Bend, Arizona. There she'd learned to ride, rope, shoot, smoke cigars, maneuver four wheel drive vehicles through arroyos and up steep canyon trails, run rivers, and in general keep up with the cowboy of whom she was so enamored.

After two years of ranch life she left the cowboy and moved to Tucson, where she worked in an art gallery. Within a year she opened her own small gallery and did so well that she opened another, larger, one in Phoenix. On a vacation in Port Tropique she was so taken with the place that she decided to open a gallery there, and now divided her time among the three galleries.

Franz was on his fifth or sixth shot of Old Overholt and fourth Noche Buena when Nathan invited Jane and Manuel to join them. He could see that Jane was a good-looking lady but he could not bring himself to speak to her. He sat and drank and heard but did not listen to the three-way conversation, motioning every so often to Alfonso to bring him another shot or another beer or both.

How it was that he and Jane had ended up in bed together that night he never could quite figure out. Franz had a vague memory of a fistfight and a lot of white shirts pushing and shoving and shouting and then he and Jane running together through the rain.

By morning he was entirely sober and sitting in the kitchen of a house he assumed belonged to Jane drinking coffee and staring at a sliced papaya and a piece of toast on a plate in front of him. Jane sat across the table wearing a bright green dress chattering on about the time she had worked as an extra in a movie being shot outside Tucson, a western starring the famous actor Warner Nolan.

Nolan asked her to dinner, she said, and she had gone to his hotel. He was the vainest man she had ever met, so afraid of *not* being recognized in public that he ate dinner every night in his hotel room rather than risk this reverse embarrassment. Jane had gone to bed with him and afterwards was furious at herself for having done so.

"He was so conceited," she said. "He just *assumed* I'd do it, and afterwards he said he'd call a cab for me. He never even got out of bed to say goodnight, just said he was tired and that I'd better be going if I wanted to get enough sleep before the next day's shooting."

"He was right, though," said Franz.

"What?"

"You did sleep with him."

"It still makes me angry when I think about it. I know

59

I've only myself to blame, but the real thing that bothers me is that I never got to find out whether or not he wears a hairpiece."

Jane continued talking throughout breakfast, then raced around getting her things together for the early flight to the States. She didn't seem to be at all concerned about the impending takeover of the country by Raoul de Avila.

"From everything I've heard he's a supporter of the arts. There's no reason why his reforms should affect my business. After all, he did graduate from Yale or some place, didn't he?"

Franz helped Jane carry her bags to her car and she offered to drop him somewhere on her way to the airport but Franz said he would walk home, it wasn't far. She kissed him quickly, got in and drove off.

He walked up to the zócalo and sat down on a bench. It began to rain lightly, then more heavily, then stopped. He sat on the wet bench until the rain started again, then got up and ran over to The Habana. He sat at a table and Alfonso came over.

"Buenos dias, señor," Alfonso said. "Señor Nathan was looking for you."

"What happened in here last night, Alfonso? Was there a fight?"

"Si, señor, a big one. Some Raoulistas insulted some loyalistas. You left with the big señora, yes?"

"Yes."

"Señor Santos, I think he was very upset."

"I don't know him."

"Would you like a coffee?"

"Is it still morning?"

"Only for a few more minutes, señor."

"Wait a few minutes, Alfonso, then bring me a Noche Buena."

You're no writer," said Nathan.

"What do you mean?" asked Franz.

"When do you work? You never work."

"All the time. Writers work all the time. They're always working, that's what Gertrude Stein said."

"Fuck Gertrude Stein."

Franz couldn't say anything to that.

"What happened with the big señora the other night?" Nathan asked.

"She took me home and fucked me, I guess."

"You guess?"

"Yeah, I guess."

Nathan laughed.

"Did Alfonso tell you how pissed off that guy Santos was?"

"I don't know him."

"Stealing a man's date in a place like this is bad business, boy. Especially Yankee nookie like that."

"I didn't plan it."

"Well, author, I have a feeling there's going to be one big blowout around these parts pretty soon. You'll have more interesting stuff than Benjamin Franklin to write about after that."

Franz finished his beer and stood up.

"There's nothing more interesting to write about than Benjamin Franklin," he said.

He was about to leave for the old dock and had just taken his jacket and the suitcase out of the closet when there was a knock at the door. Franz stuck one of the guns in his pants pocket, wrapped the other in the jacket and asked who was there.

"Rodriguez."

Franz opened up but left the big ugly bear standing outside. It was raining softly on the bear's brown fedora.

"What is it?"

"The pick-up is off for tonight but Renaldo wants to see you."

"Why didn't he come himself?"

"He wants you to meet him at El Pájaro."

"Why there?"

"That's where he is."

"Wait a minute," Franz said, shutting the door.

He took the gun out of his pants pocket and put it under the pillow on the bed. He put on the jacket and stuck the gun that was wrapped in it into one of the pockets, then he opened the door and went out.

"Did you hear how Rubio bought it?" Rodriguez asked as they walked.

"Who's Rubio?"

"The Cuban nigger used to work the bolita for the governor. You know, the tough one with the red eyes all the time."

"I don't remember him."

"Well, he was in the crapper and when he flushed it a bomb went off." Rodriguez giggled. "They said he must of took two or three shits before he pulled the chain. How do you like that? Not only was he a creep but he was an unsanitary creep."

"Maybe he was just trying to conserve water," said Franz.

El Pájaro was a fancy bar at the top of the Hotel Tropique, a roof garden with plants with big leaves between the tables. It was a tourist joint but now that the tourists were gone nobody went there but businessmen and mafiosi. Since it was raining Renaldo was sitting at the long bar under the canopy.

"There has been a change in plans," he said, rotating his neck and shoulders.

Franz sat on the next stool and ordered a Bahia. The bear grabbed an iron chair in out of the rain, wiped the seat with a handkerchief, and sprawled himself over it.

"They are going to carry a double load this trip," said the snake, "so it is taking longer. It will not affect you, they will just use larger bills."

Franz sipped at the Bahia but the sweetness made him shudder so he handed it to Rodriguez who finished half of it with one swallow.

"When do you suppose it will be here?" asked Franz.

"In two days, Miercoles. Wednesday. Unless you hear differently go out the same time as tonight. Todo es bueno? No problemas?"

"No problemas."

"Muy bien. Hasta luego."

Since El Serpiente did not get up Franz assumed it was himself who was leaving, so he did. Riding down in the elevator Franz thought about Rubio and the exploding toilet, as it had been intended he should.

As a child, Franz often accompanied his father when he called on wholesale liquor accounts outside of the city. These trips to New Iberia or Shreveport or Lake Charles were usually made during the winter, and Franz grew fond of riding in the car looking out at the farms and bayous and small towns as his father whistled "The Bonny Blue Flag" and chainsmoked Camels. They rarely spoke while his father drove, so that the boy's concentration on passing images was largely undisturbed. Even now Franz could conjure instantly the picture of a black dog shaking off the rain in front of a peeling white board fence in Plaquemines Parish about 1946.

In Houma, he remembered, was Mama Sugar's, where they'd stop for ribs, and near Morgan City was Abshire's Shrimp Shack, where deviled crabs cost three cents, two for a nickel. It was outside Abshire's that Franz saw his first dead man. There was a string of barber shops in the shanties alongside the Shrimp Shack and one of the barbers had slit somebody's throat with a razor in an argument over a craps game. Franz's father and the cops had stood around on the boardwalk eating deviled crabs and making jokes about how a man had to be careful where he got shaved these days. Both the barber and the dead man were colored so nobody was very concerned about the situation. The barber was handcuffed and put into the back of a mule-drawn police wagon they must have been using since the '20s. The dead man was left where he had fallen, lying half off the boardwalk, his dark blood dripping into the mud.

Franz and his mother had lived for a time in the house his grandmother owned in Miami Beach, before Miami Beach became what it became, and then they had lived in the old Delmonico Hotel after his grandmother sold the house. After Franz's mother married her second husband and he was seven years old, they moved to Key West, where they lived in a white hotel on the beach. Because of the heat white was the predominant shade— the sand, the glare, clothing. The hotel was large but intimate in that there were never very many guests staying in it at any one time.

Franz had had the run of the place. Whenever he caught a good eating fish in the ocean or the Gulf, a king or a grouper, he'd wrap it in newspaper and take it to the kitchen and give it to the chef, who would prepare it for him and his mother and her husband for lunch or dinner. He'd already caught quite a few large fish by the time he was seven—his first was a barracuda off Miami when he was five. Kingfish was best, filleted with just the right amount of salt, butter and garlic.

There was a canopied swing on the beach set between a pair of high coconut palms whose trunks curved like Lena Horne's body in the picture of her on the cover of the record album of the musical *Jamaica*. The hotel pool was a fenced-in area of the Atlantic. Every morning before the pool was opened to the guests, the lifeguard would swim underwater and check out the wire cage that was the swimming boundary to see that no sharks or barracuda or jellyfish or men-of-war had poked their way through during the night. His mother liked to swim in the unprotected water and was several times stung severely by jellyfish. One of Franz's favorite occupations was to walk along the beach popping men-of-war with a board and watching the blue juice spurt out over the white sand.

One evening a Conch was fishing off the long pier

behind the hotel and hooked an octopus, which somehow maneuvered itself beneath the pier and caught the line in such a way that the only way the octopus could be brought up was directly through the planks. Franz stood and watched while another Conch got a saw and cut a hole in the midole of the pier large enough for his partner to bring the octopus onto the wharf. Then he nailed the section back down.

A wonderful place in Key West was the aquarium, which had huge sea turtles, sharks and a giant jewfish within touching range. Admission was a quarter but the Seminole Indian who took the money let Franz in free because he came every day and stayed longer than even those people who came in for the first time. That aquarium, which was right on the water, and the reptile farm in St. Augustine were his favorite Florida places. He and his mother once visited the reptile farm at five in the morning when they were driving to Atlanta and persuaded the caretaker to admit them, even though it was several hours until it opened to the public. The caretaker had held Franz up over a pit full of poisonous snakes and asked him if he'd be afraid to get in there with them. The man had told Franz how when he'd worked in the turpentine camps he used to chop up cottonmouths and rattlers and cook them for supper. He'd spent as much time in those camps, he said, killing snakes as tapping trees.

Franz and his mother went many times to see the alligator wrestling. He loved to watch the gators thrown on their backs and the Indian boys rub their bellies with sand until they'd fall asleep stretched out with their tiny legs up in the air and powerful long tails absolutely still. Awakened with a slap, they'd twist over violently and hiss and slide slickly into the shallow pool provided for them. After Franz and his mother had been away for a few months they went back and found Johnny, a Seminole who'd been the chief attraction as a wrestler, watering the bird cages. Franz asked him why he wasn't with the alligators and he showed them his left hand, which was missing three fingers. He hadn't pulled it away cleanly the last time. He'd lost them to a croc, he said, which he rarely wrestled because their long, narrow jaws were more difficult to grasp firmly than the broad snout of an alligator. Now he swept up.

It was at the reptile farm in St. Augustine that Franz saw the alligators being fed. There were about thirty or forty of them piled on and around each other at the edge of a muddy pond. The caretaker threw large hunks of raw meat at the pile and the gators clambered and clawed their way over and under the others to get at it. The gators couldn't see or smell the meat right in front of them, but would attempt to wrench a chunk out of the jaws of a beast to one side, often crunching down on another's snout with its enormous teeth.

Days in Key West back then were quiet and hot but with that soothing tropical breeze Franz used always to imagine coming from Cuba. Radio Havana blared from porches along Margaret Street, and at sunset the water glistened pink under a translucent sky. It often seemed as if hardly a summer would pass, let alone the third of a century since he'd lived there.

The siege of Port Tropique began in the early evening of the day Franz was to make his third pick-up. He went up onto the roof of his house and watched the powder flashes and listened to the rifle fire and grenade blasts. As the light waned the explosions became more brilliant and beautiful. White, red, yellow and blue flashes illumined the landscape. He could see people running in the streets but could not hear any voices so he did not know if they were celebrating or fleeing in fear of the approaching rebel army. They could have waited, Franz thought. They had taken this long to get here, why couldn't they have held off for a few more days?

Franz went back inside and sat in his room listening to the guns. It sounded like the action was pitched on the other side of the city, at the outer boundary of the Montejo. If the regulars could hold them there for a while he could get to the dock without any trouble. The question was whether the serpent would risk it. If the shipment were in he had to move it, though. They couldn't chance having it confiscated by Raoul, that would be the end of it, at least for now. If Rodriguez or some other monkey didn't come to tell him it was off he would go, there was no choice.

By a quarter to nobody had shown up so Franz loaded both pieces, stuck one in each jacket pocket, picked up the suitcase, and headed for the wharf.

The boat was late, but the fighting was still pretty far off so Franz didn't panic. The citizens were going nuts out there but nobody had paid him any attention. So far as he could tell The Habana and the other cafés and bars were open. People were running around with babies in their arms yelling at each other to hurry up but he couldn't tell where they were headed. Port Tropique was the end of the line, the rest of the country had already fallen to the rebels, there was no place for loyalistas anywhere.

When he first heard the boat engine Franz thought it was a series of distant explosions, but when he looked out at the water, he could see the white hull approaching and he became excited. Renaldo threw him the line and the standard procedure was followed. The only difference was that when Franz was handed back the suitcase he was told to hold it until he received word of when to make the drop. Nothing was certain, hissed El Serpiente, now that those fleas of the dog had spread to the owner.

"Vamonos!" the snake shouted as he leaped aboard. "Andale! Andale!"

Franz watched the boat roar away and then turned and walked slowly toward the sounds of battle.

There was twice as much as usual in the suitcase this time but Franz was less nervous about carrying it than ever. He walked up the Calle Santa Cruz to The Habana and sat down at a table against the wall with the long mirror. Alfonso came over with a bottle of Bushmill's and two glasses and sat down and poured them each a drink. He put the bottle on the table and held up his glass.

"Viva Raoul!" he said.

"'Viva!" said Franz.

They downed their shots and Alfonso poured them each another.

"Viva la causa!" said Alfonso.

"Viva!" said Franz.

They downed the whisky and sat listening to the gunfire. Citizens ran by in both directions.

"La gente are restless," said Franz.

Alfonso filled both glasses again.

"Have you seen Señor Nathan?" Franz asked.

Alfonso drank up.

"No, señor. He is with the fighting probablemente."

"Quel journaliste," said Franz, then he drank up too.

"Where you go with the suitcase, señor? All the roads are blockaded."

A tank rumbled past the café followed by two jeeps full of Nacionalistas holding FN rifles.

"Better you stay and drink whisky with me, señor. Is free. Is revolution. People free. Whisky free." He poured two more. "Otro vez!"

Just then a very large explosion rocked the café. Tables and chairs fell over. The long mirror cracked in half but did not shatter.

Alfonso drank up quickly.

"Very close, señor. Very good mirror," he said.

"To the end of another beautiful dictatorship," said Franz, holding up his glass.

He knocked it back and stood up.

"You go anyway, señor?"

"Thank you, Alfonso," Franz said, holding out his hand. "It is a pleasure to know you and I hope you will have many fine children."

Alfonso shook Franz's hand.

"Mil gracias, señor. Cuidado."

Franz picked up the suitcase with one hand and with the other spread flat waved goodbye like he'd seen James Dean do in *Giant*.

Franz kept walking west on Calle Cincuenta Uno until it hit the zoo. The animals were raving, clawing away and banging their bloodied heads and bodies against the bars and doors of their cages. Each new explosion sent the beasts into raging fits. The tigers were especially crazed, trying to squeeze themselves between the bars, rubbing off their fur. Franz wished he had the keys to the cages and a way to avoid being mauled and trampled after he let them out.

At the park he saw government troops running south, away from the direction of the battle. After they had passed Franz ran into the park and leaned against a tree. He lit the last of his Cuban cigars. After he had puffed on it a few times he bent down and opened the suitcase to make sure it really was a half-million dollars in cash he was lugging around.

He knelt and looked at the money. He puffed on the cigar. Then he laughed. He laughed and laughed and fell on the ground and rolled around in the wet leaves. The animals growled and honked and shrieked, the guns bopped and chattered and Franz lay on the ground and laughed and cried and then began to shiver and shake and vomit and crap and piss until he had nothing left in him and he passed out.

When Franz awoke it was still dark. He was cold and shaky but he managed to get to his feet and start walking. After he'd gone ten steps he stopped and went back for the suitcase. There was no gunfire but he could hear horrible noises still coming from the zoo like it was the operating room of Doctor Moreau.

He continued walking west until he came to a road running north and south. To the north and west were Uxpan and Domingo City. To the south was Mipam, a donkey crossing, and thick jungle all the way to the Tampeche border.

Franz headed north, sticking to the road until he heard a vehicle approaching, then hiding in the woods and continuing on after it had passed. The only traffic consisted of trucks and jeeps. Franz couldn't tell which side they belonged to but he assumed they were Raoulistas.

By the time he reached the outskirts of Uxpan the sky was beginning to get light. Franz had no idea how long it had taken him to get that far and he walked up the main road through the town. Nothing was moving, not even the chickens around the whorehouse. A yellow dog lying under an old Chevrolet chassis up on blocks opened one red eye for a moment then closed it again.

Franz knew where he was headed now and he trudged on. A white ambulance sped by in the direction of Port Tropique so fast that he didn't even have time to hide in the bushes. It began to rain steadily then and the light remained vague. He turned in at the white stone drive and kept going until he got to the car, pushed the suitcase underneath, crawled in after it and collapsed.

It was the Indian woman who found him. She saw his hand sticking out and ran for help.

"Young man, young man, are you all right? What are you doing under there?"

Franz opened his eyes and saw a woman on her hands and knees with her head on one side almost against the ground. It was Frau Kroner.

"Are you all right?" she repeated.

He crawled out, pulling the suitcase along after him. Frau Kroner and the Indian woman helped him to his feet and inside the house. He noticed that it was drizzling.

When Franz awakened next he was in a bed wearing clean clothes. Other than the fact that he was unshaven he appeared to himself to be in respectable condition. He was alone in a room behung with brightly colored tapestries of Indian design. He got up and took one step and sat down on the bed. The soles of his feet were covered with blisters so he stood up and walked on the sides of them as best he could into the front room where he and Nathan had first been asked to wait. The Indian woman saw him and guided him out to the terrace where Max Kroner's widow was writing in a notebook. It had stopped raining but the sky was full of clouds.

"Mr. Hall, is it not?" said the Frau, looking up.

Franz nodded.

"Please sit down and have some coffee. Teresa makes wonderful coffee."

Franz sat down and in a moment the Indian woman brought him a cup of hot coffee.

"Where is the suitcase?" he asked.

"In the vestibule there, near the door. Are you feeling any better?"

"I think so. My feet are sore."

"Go ahead and drink."

Franz drank some of the coffee.

74

"I walked here from Port Tropique."

"Why?"

"No other way to come."

"But why did you leave?"

"It got pretty crazy there last night. The rebels came in smoking. Didn't they stop here?"

"No. There would be no reason for them to. They have been passing on the road for the last two days."

"Do you know what the situation is in Domingo?"

"I am told it is better now. Is that where you want to go?"

"I want to get to the States if it's possible."

"I have heard there are to be special flights out for foreigners, but I do not know when."

Franz drank the rest of his coffee.

"Frau Kroner," he said, "thank you for taking me in, for cleaning me up. I must have been a mess."

Frau Kroner smiled. "You stank like a mule," she said. Franz laughed.

"If I might ask you another favor. Could you possibly give me a ride to Domingo City? It's important that I get on one of those flights as soon as possible."

"Yes, I can drive you if you like. Would you like to go now or do you want something to eat first?"

"No, thank you." Franz stood up. "I would like to pay you for the clothes."

Frau Kroner shook her head. "Please take them, they were Max's. I have no use for them except on those rare occasions when it is necessary to provide wardrobes for strange pilgrims who sleep beneath automobiles."

The streets of Ciudad Domingo were crowded. Everyone was celebrating, drinking, firing pistols in the air. The news had been received confirming the rebel victory in Port Tropique. Raoul de Avila was El Presidente.

"Viva Raoul!" people shouted at them as they drove by. "Viva El Presidente!"

Frau Kroner drove through the city directly to the airport.

"What happened to your friend?" she asked. "Mr. Nathan, the journalist."

"I don't know. He must still be in Port Tropique, reporting on the revolution."

"For some reason I have never been fond of reporters," said Frau Kroner. "Nor writers in general. Both Max and I always found them ultimately to be extremely selfish people. You are not a writer, are you, Mr. Hall?"

"No," said Franz, "I'm not."

At the airport he insisted that Frau Kroner leave him, even though there would be no plane leaving for several hours. It was a flight to Galveston for United States citizens only.

"I'll be fine," Franz said. "Thank you for everything."

"I hope you will return someday, Mr. Hall. Things will be difficult for a while, but at least now there is hope."

She waved then and drove away. Franz watched her red convertible until it was out of sight. The old girl is right, he thought. Things will be difficult for a while, but at least now there is hope.

Pancho Villa never told anyone his plans. When his troops bedded down for the night Villa would hand his horse over to an orderly, wrap himself in a serápe and walk off into the dark and reappear the next morning from a different direction. Before he went to work for Madero as a Captain, then as a General, when he was still a bandit, Villa would make camp with a companion, then pretend to sleep until he could steal away unnoticed and ride all night in the direction in which he was least likely to be followed.

Franz watched the other passengers board the airplane. He waited until it had taken off and then hired a taxi to drive him to the railroad station in Ciudad Domingo. He bought a ticket to Istmo Delgado de las Palmas in Tampeche and sat down to wait for the train, which, he was informed by the drunken Raoulista stationmaster, was going to be a few hours later than the scheduled two hours behind the arrival listed on the timetable.

Villa would approve of this tactic, thought Franz. From Istmo Delgado he would be able to get a boat to anywhere, and now nobody knew where to find him.

It took seven hours by steam locomotive from Domingo City to Istmo Delgado. Franz slept most of the way. The rest of the time he silently and fascinatedly observed the passengers holding live chickens, small pigs, fish and children, lots of children. Since the Rockefeller Foundation began its immunization program the children in South and Central America survived. Everywhere were children, the place was overrun by kids. The third world, Franz could not help but acknowledge, was burgeoning.

The train wound slowly, almost idly, through the jungle. Every so often the engineer would stop so that overgrown roots could be hacked away from the tracks. At the Tampeche border authorities came aboard and checked visa cards. Franz offered his passport but the guard, seeing the United States emblem, brushed it aside and did not even bother to inspect or stamp it. From the border to Istmo Delgado was not very far and Franz was glad when the train finally emerged from the forest and came into the open. The city was at the tip of a needlepoint strip of beach and Franz was thankful for the ocean breeze as the train approached the end of the land.

Because of its numerous coves, lagoons and inlets Tampeche had long been a favorite haunt of pirates and other renegades, resulting in the most common surnames of its inhabitants being Morgan and Jones. The mahogany having long since been stripped from the interior, the only remaining industries belonged to the Coca-Cola Company and United Fruit, whose directors conspired to keep Tampeche the poorest country in Central America.

Istmo Delgado de las Palmas was a small coastal town most of whose citizens worked as fishermen. The rest who worked did so either in the Coca-Cola plant or on the banana docks for wages which amounted to next to nothing. There was a somnolent atmosphere about the place, a marked contrast to the revolutionary fervor of Port Tropique, and it seemed to Franz, especially in light of Tampeche's reputation as a fugitives' haven, an ideal spot to hole up in for a while.

From the porch of the bungalow Franz could watch the waves roll in and the shore fishermen snare with their nets the smelt attempting to deposit their eggs in the gravel. The palms were bending in the soft steady wind and the air was redolent with a sweet blend of fruit and sea. Franz felt as if he had been rescued from the real world.

He spent the days walking on the beach, swimming in the warm ocean and drinking piña coladas. Except for an occasional evening in an open air fishermen's bar Franz kept to himself. He began to keep a journal, not a diary but a book of remarks, reminiscences and dreams.

As usual it was Marie who at first dominated his thoughts, but it was a vision of Max Kroner that gradually insinuated itself and at last came clearly into focus and took hold. With the help of his wife Kroner had resurrected himself in the face of professional disfavor and alcoholism. Unlike Hilda and Max, however, Franz knew that Marie had given up on him.

What good was the money, he thought. There was no point to his trying to get away with it. If he brought it back it would be all right, they might not kill him. He had become frightened during the rebel attack, that's all, he had panicked. He hadn't wanted the Raoulistas to find him so he had gone into hiding until the situation calmed down. He had never intended to steal it. He would go back, he decided. He would find out what was happening there and as soon as the time seemed right he would take the money back to Port Tropique.

The day after Franz had made the decision to return to Port Tropique he wired a thousand dollars to his mother, which left him more than three thousand from the two successful drops. That would be plenty, he figured, until he made contact with Renaldo and the operation started up again.

Walking away from the telegraph office Franz got the feeling that someone was following him. He didn't turn around until he had crossed two streets, then he stopped and lit a cigaret. A barefoot man in the standard Tampeche outfit of white pants and shirt and straw sombrero sat on his haunches at the curb and looked away. Franz continued on and looked back a couple of times but the man was not there.

That night a scraping noise startled Franz from a dream wherein Max Kroner was instructing him in the skinning of an alligator. Marie had been sitting in a chair completely naked holding an open black umbrella and smiling. He saw the man in white but without the sombrero kneeling with his back to the bed attempting to pick the lock on the suitcase which he had slid out from underneath the large chest of drawers next to the window. Franz took the .32 from under his pillow.

"Ladrón!" he said quietly, and as the man began to turn and pick up the machete that lay by his right foot Franz shot him twice in the head.

The police in Istmo Delgado were pretty much like police anywhere except that they wore fancier uniforms. Officials in Central and South American countries are crazy about costumes because they separate them from the ordinary citizens and make more obvious their roles as authorities.

Franz answered their questions about the shooting as simply and straightforwardly as possible, avoiding only the contents of the suitcase which the intruder had not succeeded in prying open before being killed. There was no reason for anyone to know what was in there, only that the ladrón had broken and entered and had for his trouble ended up dead on the floor of Franz's bedroom.

There was nothing complicated about any of it. The man had seen Franz send one thousand dollars at the telegraph office and followed him in order to find out where he was staying and then come back that night in order to steal whatever remaining cash or other valuables he could find.

It quickly became obvious to Franz that the only way it would be possible to avoid further inquiry into the case was for him to furnish a generous mordida then and there. He took each of the three polizontes individually onto the porch and gave them five twenty dollar bills after which they collectively agreed that the case was cut and dried and required no further investigation. Since any person of means in Tampeche carried or kept a weapon of some kind no mention was made as to the reason for Franz's possession of a pistol.

An ambulance wagon was sent for and after the attendants had removed the body the carabiñeros expressed to Franz their profuse and abundant apologies for the unforgivable behavior of their deceased countryman. Even in the United States, they averred, there must occur an occasional aberrant incident of this nature. They assured Franz that this would be the only untoward experience to befall him while he was in residence in Istmo Delgado, or for that matter in all of Tampeche, tipped several times and with great ceremony the sparkling black brims of their spaghetti-draped caps, and went out.

As soon as they had gone Franz began to gather up his belongings for the journey.

Because of the uncertain political situation at the present time trains were not running into Ciudad Domingo. The airports, too, were closed. The only way he could get to Port Tropique, Franz learned, other than overland through the jungle, was by boat. The banana freighters were still scheduling calls at Tropique but even in the best of times it was difficult to unload a passenger because of the number of bribes required. The best bet, the bartender at the fishermen's bar informed Franz, was to pay someone who owned their own boat to take him there.

The situation reminded Franz of Harry Morgan's attempts to illegally transport first twelve Chinese from Bacuranao to Florida and then four rebel Cubans from Key West to Havana in *To Have and Have Not*. The Cubans wound up dead at sea and the Chinese never made it out of Cuba. Harry Morgan didn't do very well by himself either. But it appeared to be the only acceptable solution so Franz gave the bartender five dollars and by late afternoon he had been introduced to a fisherman named Bernardo Mendoza-Morgan who agreed to take him that night for a hundred dollars.

The trip was not a long one, only three hours straight up the coast, but very dangerous, Bernardo told Franz, if they should be discovered by a patrol boat. Bernardo's craft was hardly more than a glorified dinghy with a small motor so it would be impossible to conceal a passenger from the Tropique shore police. The Raoulistas would think they were loyalist troublemakers and execute them on the spot. If they were intercepted by Nacionalistas they could hardly expect more generous treatment. But a hundred United States dollars was more than Bernardo could expect to make in six months as a fisherman and so he was willing to take the chance.

He told Franz he would drop him on the southern reach of a tiny peninsula about six miles from Port

Tropique. From there Franz would have to walk. The thought of another long hike made Franz grimace but he agreed to the plan and gave Bernardo twenty-five dollars. He would give him another twenty-five when he came aboard and the second fifty when they arrived at their destination. Franz showed Bernardo the rest of the money and told him not to worry, they would be more fortunate than the characters in a book he had read had been. After all, Franz said, laughing, he and Bernardo were real men.

Bernardo said he hoped Franz was right, but that even though he could not read he knew it was only real men who could die and not the characters in a book.

It was a clear night, the rain had come in the early evening and Franz remarked to Bernardo, about how fortunate they were to have such marvelous visibility and so would not be likely to crack up on a reef or run aground on a sandbar.

Bernardo, however, did not think they were so fortunate and in fact almost suggested that they postpone the trip until there was as little visibility as possible. The fog would conceal them, he explained to Franz. Under a clear sky like this one they could be as easily spotted as the reefs. But Bernardo would feel better the sooner the thing was finished and he and Franz set out at the appointed hour.

They did not talk much. Both of them were nervous and kept watching for patrol cruisers. So far as Franz had been able to find out, Raoul's forces were controlling the country, but Torres was expected to launch a counter insurgency from the loyalist retreat just across the western border in Puerto Redondo. There was apparently no fighting going on in either of the two major cities, Ciudad Domingo or Port Tropique, at the moment, and what activities there were consisted of minor skirmishes in rural border settlements to which many loyalists had fled. The upper classes had abandoned the country altogether and were temporarily relocated in Mexico City or Miami.

After an hour or more Franz realized he had been clutching tightly the handle of the suitcase the entire time and his hand was numb. He released it carefully and put his hand for a moment into the warm current. The seas were keeping at two to three feet and Bernardo's little boat chugged steadily and surprisingly, to Franz, quietly along. There were no lights along this part of the shoreline and the foliage resembled a long black scarf lying rumpled on a marble table in front of a midnight blue, silver-speckled wall.

"Mira!" said Bernardo, pointing to starboard.

There was a ship flying Panamanian colors less than a quarter of a mile off heading south-southeast at about twelve knots.

"Let's hope that's the only kind of vessel we see," said Franz, and Bernardo nodded.

They continued undisturbed and slightly over an hour later they sighted the peninsula. Franz handed Bernardo the fifty dollars.

"If we don't make it now," he said, "it won't make any difference."

When they were close enough, Bernardo cut the engine and let the boat drift in with the tide. Listening to the waves slap at them Franz envisioned himself with Marie in a rowboat on Lake Ponchartrain the time Marie thought she saw a bloated corpse floating on the water. She had wanted Franz to row over to it but he had laughed at her and gone in the opposite direction. After they had docked the boat Marie told the harbor guard about the body and he had just pointed to the NO SWIMMING sign posted that day and mumbled something about people always having to learn the hard way.

After Franz was safely ashore Bernardo started the motor and headed out as fast as he could go. Franz stood for a minute watching him buck the tide before he turned and began walking along the beach toward Port Tropique.

He thought about where he should go. There might still be a room on Calle Cincuenta Ocho but El Serpiente or Rodriguez or one of the others had probably already been there and scared the shit out of everybody. That wouldn't do. He needed time to explain the circumstances and it would be better to make contact in public. But that will come later, he thought, now I need a place to stay.

Franz remembered that the border guard who had come aboard the train at Tampeche had not stamped his passport, so he wouldn't have to invent a story about re-entering the country. At least he would be spared that difficulty. The Raoulistas would be doubly suspicious of any gringos still in Port Tropique.

Perhaps The Habana was open. But he didn't want to go in there with the suitcase again. He didn't want to be seen carrying it through the streets either, but there was nothing to do about it unless he buried it someplace. That would be tough without a shovel and even if he could do it what if somebody found the spot and dug it up or the rains soaked through? No, he'd hang on to it and march right on into town and act as if there were nothing wrong. After all, it wasn't the Raoulistas he was afraid of.

Franz stopped several times to rest and once slept for about an hour so that it was just past dawn when he reached the city limits. At first the only other things moving on the streets were Indian women and dogs, but as it got lighter there were more people, mostly men going to work as if the revolution had changed nothing. Maybe it hadn't, Franz thought.

He stopped at the Hotel Delicado on Calle Diez y Ocho and rented a room for two dollars a day, paying a week in advance and giving the manager ten dollars extra to see that he would not be disturbed and that no one would go into the room when he was not there.

Despite assurances from the manager as profuse and abundant as those he had received from the polizontes in Istmo Delgado, Franz knew nothing of this sort could be depended upon but felt that the additional courtesy would provide at least the possibility of his requests being honored. Once in his room Franz locked the door with the back of the chair tilted under the knob, put the suitcase under the bed and one of the revolvers under his pillow and went to sleep.

In the dream Marie was standing at the sink in the hotel room in Sapporo washing out her underwear, a towel wrapped around like a little skirt, while he sat in a chair by the window. The door opened and two women and two men came in. The men had beards and were wearing suits and the women had shiny black hair and long, dangling earrings but none of them had recognizable faces.

Franz picked up a high-powered rifle from the window ledge, carefully sighted the people and shot them each several times in the forehead and chest. Marie was singing a familiar song from some '40s or '50s musical but Franz couldn't remember the name of it. There were autographed pictures of old-time baseball players on the walls and a blue velvet leopard head above the bed.

When Franz awoke the room was filled with a strong white light that reminded him of Bimini. He had gone with his Uncle Buck to Nassau to help crew a friend's yawl to Marathon Key and they had stopped at Bimini to fuel the emergency outboard and take on fresh water before continuing across the Gulf Stream. It was February, and though the light was intense the temperature and humidity were moderate, making the day comfortable.

Two old black men had been sitting on the jetty playing checkers, and Franz had stood and watched them while Buck and the skipper went up to the bar.

"Hello," said one of them. "How you today?"

"Fine," Franz said.

"I am Uncle Jim," said the man, "and this—" he pointed to his opponent, "is Doctor Jim."

Doctor Jim, a wrinkled, emaciated little man with a cotton swab of fuzzy hair, smiled and nodded.

"You in on the Morgan boat," said Uncle Jim.

"That's right," Franz answered. "How did you know it was a Morgan?"

Uncle Jim laughed. "Oh, I know most the boats. Them Morgans is mighty good."

Doctor Jim made a move and Uncle Jim nodded, smiling his yellow teeth and yellow eyes before executing a double jump.

"Crown me, papa, crown me!" he shouted.

Doctor Jim got up, picked his cane off the bench, nodded to Franz, and hobbled away.

"You tired fish these days!" Uncle Jim hollered after him.

Uncle Jim stood up. He was over six feet tall but his stooped shoulders made him shorter. Franz figured he was close to seventy years old.

"Bet you think how old I am," he said. "Ha, ha. I am eighty-two July. Still strong. I know Hemingway here, we box on dock. He knock me out. You know Hemingway?"

"I know of him," said Franz. "His books."

"Ha, ha. That some fella Hemingway. Haven't seen him in many years."

"He's dead," Franz told Uncle Jim. "He shot himself in 1961."

Uncle Jim nodded. "Good reason why I no longer see him. I not really been waiting anyhow."

The first place he headed was The Habana. There were small groups of rebel soldiers in the streets, usually four to six men walking slowly and talking rapidly. Others went by in American-made jeeps. Large picture posters of Raoul were on every wall with the word "ARRIBA!" scrawled under his photograph in red. At each corner of the zócalo fruits and vegetables were being dispensed from the backs of trucks free of charge to citizens lined up to receive them. Everyone seemed very happy except for the shoeshine boys, who did not appear to be doing much business.

The Habana was open. Franz spotted Alfonso behind the bar and went over and shook his hand.

"Hola, amigo," he said.

"Bienvenido!" said Alfonso. "It is good to see you again. What may I serve you?"

"Have you still got everything?"

"Si, señor, everything that is not gone."

"How about coffee with a shot of Irish in it?"'

"No problema. Will you be staying long this time in Port Tropique?"

"It depends on how things go in the country."

Alfonso set down the coffee.

"It is a free country now, señor, but we have no milk."

"What was it before," said Franz, "when you had milk?"

Alfonso laughed and poured himself a half shot of Bushmill's.

"Salúd!" he said. "It is good to see an old customer again!"

Franz held up his cup and took a sip as Alfonso swallowed the whisky.

"Señor Nathan is staying at the Consuelo," said Alfonso.

"Why not the Tropique?"

"That is government now. El Presidente's headquarters

are on the top floor and the rest is occupied by soldiers."

"Well, now the people have a president who is an aristocrat and a socialist instead of a governor who is half Indian and a fascist."

"I am not so sure the governor was half of an Indian. I think probablemente he was all of an Indian, otherwise he would not have closed down las casas de putas."

"Have you seen Renaldo, the one who looks like a snake? Or his pal, el oso grande?"

"No, señor. Since Raoul is in the city there is no room for them."

Franz finished the coffee.

"Thanks, Alfonso. I think I'll look up the periodista."

"It is fine you are back, señor. Perhaps the revolution will not put too many of us out of work."

"Let us hope," said Franz, and they shook hands again.

Earl Bell was a free-lance reporter and photographer from Atlanta who had interviewed Les Duvalier (père et fils), Trujillo and his boy Rubirosa, been in the Sierra Maestre with Fidel, Bolivia with Ché seen Allende's assassination, Marcos's wife stabbed, and Saigon fall. He was in Port Tropique to do an "inside" story on Raoul de Avila but had been unable, as he admitted to Paul Nathan and Franz, to get inside.

"He's either a stone paranoid son of a bitch or a real red," Bell said. "Maybe both."

"Could be he's just too busy," suggested Franz.

Bell laughed. "Maybe. But I think more likely he's got a deal with the Chinks. They pay his way and tell him what to say and who to say it to, just like them Africans what was weaned on Radio Peking. He knows I know it and that's why I can't get in there."

"Franz said he saw some American make jeeps this morning," said Nathan.

"Copped from the loyalists. Raoul's a Chinese bandit."

"That's what Paul Dietzel used to call his defensive team at LSU," said Franz. "The Chinese Bandits."

"Well I don't know if our Raoul can keep his boys number one as long as Dietzel did his," said Bell. "That's why I want to get to him right now, before Chinkthink decides he ain't doin' the job right, or some other benevolent servant of the people gets it in his head to deck him."

The three of them sat and talked and drank beers in the bar of the Consuelo until Bell decided to give it another try and headed off to the Tropique.

"How about you?" Franz asked Nathan. "The *Post* still paying the bills?"

"They want me to stick around a little while longer, see if Raoul holds the fort." He sucked on a Superior.

"I heard you were at the front the night of the sixth," said Franz.

"They came through like gangbusters. Torres high-tailed it in a private copter about ten minutes into the first assault. He's supposed to be rehearsing a comeback in Redondo."

"So I understand."

"Even the citizens were busting heads," said Nathan. "What happened to you?"

"I had some business in Tampeche."

Nathan nodded. "The two days after that were like one long New Year's Eve. It got pretty crazy until Raoul made a big speech in the zócalo and cooled everybody down. Told 'em it was time to go to work for themselves instead of for gangsters like the governor or Torres. They ate it up. I haven't seen Raoul since. He and his crowd commandeered the Tropique."

"I know, Alfonso told me. That's how I found you here."

"Yes sir, author, I sure am sorry you missed the fireworks."

Franz smiled. "Maybe I'll get lucky yet," he said.

Franz had dinner in The Habana that night with Nathan, Bell, and a *Newsweek* correspondent named Joanna Noyes. Bell had been unsuccessful that afternoon in his attempt to interview Raoul, so, since the airport was now open for official travel and to those with foreign passports, he was going to leave in the morning.

"I hope to get out soon myself," said Nathan. "If nothing's shaking within three or four days I'll see you up north."

"I won't be there long," said Bell. "By next week I should be on my way to do Sadat for *Playboy*. No rest for the pest!"

"And what do you do, Mr. Hall?" Joanna Noyes asked.

Nathan laughed. "Franz is a writer too," he said. "A real one. Knows all about Gertrude Stein."

"Are you working on anything in particular?" she asked.

"I was," said Franz. "But I seem to be at an impasse."

"What happened to Ben Franklin?" asked Nathan.

"Ben Franklin?" said Bell.

"Franz was writing a book about him. He said there was nothing more interesting to write about than Benjamin Franklin."

"Did you ever interview him, Mr. Bell?" said Joanna Noyes.

"Nope, but I talked to Ezra Pound when he was in the booby hatch, and that was just as good. He knew more about Franklin and Adams and Jefferson, or thought he did, than they did themselves. You all should read his book about Jefferson and Mussolini. It puts this here hill of beans in a nut."

After dinner they talked and drank for a while and when Franz saw that Nathan meant to put a move on Joanna Noyes he wished Bell luck and bade the others goodnight.

Passing through the zócalo on his way to the Delicado Franz realized that Renaldo might not wait to kill him until after the money had been recovered. Renaldo just took orders, after all, and a half million, or whatever they figured was left, wouldn't mean much to whomever gave them.

A wind started up and Franz stood and watched the flamboyanas in front of the big church bow and wave as if formally extending a Japanese farewell.

Franz suddenly had a great desire to see his Uncle Buck. It was hard to believe that he was dead, especially since Port Tropique was really Buck's kind of place.

A Douglas Fairbanks-like, as well as look-alike, adventurer, Franz's Uncle Buck had been an interesting man. At the age of twelve he'd been an assistant to Blackstone the magician. For years he'd kept his black trunk full of tricks stored in the garage behind the house in New Orleans. When Franz was a boy Buck would occasionally perform a few of them for him and his friends, but Buck would never show them how to do any except for the most elementary ones. The important disclosures could be made only to serious apprentice magicians, he explained.

He'd then established, at thirteen, his own novelties business, and saved enough money to purchase a car in order to run away from home with a gang of older boys. According to Franz's mother, who had told him the story, the boys had planned to murder Buck and dump him in a ditch outside of town, but Buck's mother found out about the plot and chased them down before it could be carried out.

As a teenager Buck rode an Indian motorcycle and did daredevil stunts at carnivals and fairs. While working his way through college he captained the fencing team and was the state amateur golfing champion. After he had graduated with two engineering degrees, Buck went off to help build the railroad through the Yukon.

"After six months I got pneumonia," he told Franz, "and was airlifted down to Seattle. After I got out of the hospital I went into a bar for a drink. I swore I'd never see the territories again. Turns out the bartender has an outfit mining iron ore out of Dawson and needs a man who knows the country to run the show, an engineer. He offered an incredible amount of money and sure enough I was on my way back up that night."

Buck constructed bridges in Ireland, Portugal and Burma, lumberjacked on Iron Mountain in Michigan, was a full Commander in the Navy during World War Two, and refused an Admiralty to return to civilian life and begin his own construction company.

He had almost been shot by the Fidelistas shortly after the revolution in Cuba because of his resemblance to a general of Batista's. The men had not fired upon him because there were too many people in the street and he was walking with an old man, his father—Franz's grandfather—whom he had taken with him to Havana to see what was going on. Castro's soldiers arrested Buck and took him to headquarters, where they showed him a picture of the General on the front page of that day's newspaper. The resemblance was remarkable, and after he'd proven his identity Buck bought a dozen copies of the paper to take home.

Franz had worked for Buck in Florida during the summers when he was a boy, laying pipe, building streets and houses. Buck would always show up at the job site in his banged-up Cadillac convertible, which he used like a pick-up truck. He'd jump down into a ditch and show everybody how to dig or hop up on a roof and demonstrate the proper way to set trusses as if nobody else had ever dug a ditch or set a truss before. Inevitably, as he was trying to drive away, Buck's car would get stuck in the mud or sand. He would scramble around in his trunk for tools or boards and Franz and the other workers would have to help push him out. The amazing thing to Franz was that despite all of his uncle's eccentricities and often unreasonable demands, people enjoyed working for him. He was slightly insane but his spirit was ingenuous.

Buck often took Franz fishing and had helped to raise him after Franz's father's death. However, after their sailing trip across the Gulf Stream, during which they were almost killed, they had seen each other infrequently and seldom corresponded, each hearing news of the other through Franz's mother, Buck's sister.

After not hearing about Uncle Buck for a particularly long spell, Franz's mother told him that Buck had bought a farm on Utila, an island off the north coast of Honduras. Since his uncle was then past sixty, Franz figured Buck had decided to take it easy in the tropics.

Soon after that the worst hurricane in the history of the western hemisphere hit Central America, and hardest hit was Honduras. The newspapers reported widespread death and destruction, followed by famine and disease. A week after the hurricane Franz had received a card postmarked La Ceiba, the mainland Honduras city nearest Utila. "Dear Nephew," it read, "Stories of Honduras highly exaggerated. Have seen only four dead, three bridges & roads out & killed two snakes trying to put oil in engine. Best, Uncle Buck."

One Friday when Franz was working for his Uncle Buck, Earl, one of the pipe layers, asked Franz if he wanted to go to a dance at night and meet some Spanish girls. Franz said that would, and about eight-thirty Earl and a friend of his named Murph picked him up.

Earl was very dark, he looked almost Spanish himself though he was anything but—he came from New Hampshire, where he'd worked in his father's plumbing business until the old man had died. Earl's mother had sold the business after that and Earl had drifted since then, doing occasional work wherever he landed. He was about forty, wore his hair in a crewcut— "Had it this way all my life," he told Franz—and chainsmoked Chesterfields. His friend Murph was quite a bit younger, near Franz's age, and didn't say much on the way to the dance hall.

At the dance Murph immediately disappeared into the crowd. He was small and dark like Earl and blended in easily. Franz could see that he and Earl and Murph were in a distinct minority. There were only a handful of non-Spanish men.

"Lots of these broads is nymphos," said Earl. "They may act like they ain't never even spuk to a fella before when ya ask em to dance, but shit, you wait till you get one alone, where they ain't got no brothers er mothers er sisters watchin' over em and sheeit, you name it."

Along one of the walls sat the girls. Prim, hands folded in their laps, eyes averted from whomsoever's stare might be directed at them. Near them sat the mothers, talking a mile a minute, tugging their too-short dresses down over their thick thighs, fluffing their home-made hair-dos with one hand while they gabbed, every so often eyeing one of the young muchachos on the dance floor, smiling whenever they caught an absent glance, as if they were the object of the young man's interest.

"See ya," said Earl, and Franz watched as he intercepted an elfin señorita on the way back to her seat and spoke to her in perfect Spanish, leading her back to the middle of the floor, and dancing. The band was a Cuban quintet that played nothing but upbeat Top 40 American tunes, sung in Spanish. One of them, a very short kid who looked about twelve, and probably was, danced continuously from one end of the stage to the other playing an enormous pair of maracas. For all of the time Franz was at the dance, the kid never stopped.

Franz walked around, looking over the girls. He briefly caught the eye of one, an unusual-looking girl with brightly painted eyebrows, huge gold earrings, and a large birthmark drawn on her right cheek. She stared at the floor. He walked over to her and asked her if she wanted to dance. She looked up at him. Her features were delicate, in startling contrast to the way she was painted up—a small, thin nose and finely curved chin, with blazing great black eyes.

"No," she said, shaking her head, and quickly looked down.

Franz stood there for a few moments, wanting to say something, but he walked away and leaned against the opposite wall, watching the girl. She looked up and down again so quickly that if he had not been staring at her he would never have seen it. They continued that way for a while, Franz looking at her looking at the floor, until he decided to try once more. Franz went over and sat next to her. He watched the kid with the maracas who looked as if he were about to catapult off the stage into the gyrating mob. Franz noticed that the girl was staring at him.

"Are you seen-seer?" she asked. "Eef you are not seen-seer I con no donce weeth you." She stared seriously at him.

"I am sincere when I say I want to dance with you."

"All right," she said.

She walked into the center of the floor and turned to him. She held her gold-buckled, black patent purse in

103

one hand, the one she put on Franz's shoulder. They danced slowly, even though the music was fast. While they were dancing, she looked straight out over his shoulder. She had a slender, deeply brown neck around which she wore an imitation pearl choker set on a piece of black velvet. A burgundy ribbon was wrapped around her large bun of hair.

"It must be very long," Franz said.

"Long?" she asked. "Wot?"

"Your hair. Is it?"

"Eet has nafer been cot."

They danced for a few minutes more before she stopped and walked toward the door. Franz was surprised, and followed her. She went out and down the stairs, stopping on the bottom step, and leaned back against one of the parked cars.

"You are seen-seer?" she asked again.

Franz looked at her.

"I haf a baby," she said.

He still looked at her.

"I haf two babies."

"Good," he said.

"Eet no ees good. I don won them. They cry."

"All babies cry," said Franz. "They have to."

"They ain my babies reely. They ain my babies reely eef I don won them."

Franz looked across the road. There was a big neon sign flashing: RIO BAR blank RIO BAR.

"I am theenking eef you fock weeth me wot weel hoppen."

"What?"

"Oh, you woan won marry me cos I haf already thees babies."

"What is your name?" asked Franz.

"Concha."

"Concha, you must take care of your babies or they will not be happy. You want to be happy, don't you?"

Concha nodded.

"Then you know your babies want also to be happy.

104

You must take good care of them. How old are you? Tiene años usted?"

"Feefteen on a hof."

"Concha, you are a beautiful girl. I am sincere when I say that. You take good care of your babies so they will grow up strong and beautiful. I am going now."

"Whar you go?"

Franz didn't answer. He walked across the road into the bar and bought a six-pack. He came out and sat in the parking lot, cracked open a beer, and took a long drink.

"Ow! Lonnie, no! No, Lonnie!"

Franz saw a woman stretched out over the hood of a white car in the rear of the lot. A man was beating her with a tire iron.

"Lonnie!"—whomp—"Lonnie!"—whomp—"You crazy bastard!"—whomp—"Oh please, Lonnie honey, I won't do it again!"—whomp—"Oh Lonnie!"—whomp —"Lon-eeeeee!"

Franz put the six-pack under his arm and walked off down the road drinking the can he'd opened. A couple of cars zoomed by but he didn't try to hitch a ride. He drained the can and tossed it into the bushes. He wanted to walk for a while.

The sight of beggars on the streets did not disturb Franz. Raoul had pledged to eradicate the necessity for begging, and given the chance he probably would, but Franz could not help but be fascinated by the beggars in Tropique just as he had been as a boy in New Orleans by the bums along the riverbank. He had liked to sit in the sun with the bums by the Mississippi and watch the tankers and tramp steamers and freighters from all over the world go by while the hobos argued, told stories, drank wine and slept. The railroad ran alongside the river there and the air smelled heavily of malt from the Jax brewery next to the tracks.

Franz watched the bums and beggars wherever he went. It was not easy to become a bum, he had decided, but once you were one, he knew, it was difficult to be anything else. Anybody could become a bum, and what interested Franz was the possibility that he could become one. The prospect did not frighten him. Sometimes he thought he really believed that it would be better to be a bum than a man with too much money.

On the cold days in New Orleans Franz liked to go in the afternoons to Tujague's on Decatur Street. There were no bums in Tujague's, just workingmen, and, since it was in the Quarter, an occasional tourist. But the whisky wasn't overpriced and the tourists rarely stayed after one drink. Mainly there were construction workers on their breaks waiting for the race results and talking sports and ladies, a few ladies with older men looking at the younger men, coffee importers complaining about the late shipment from Colombia, and sometimes a brakeman or conductor rushing in for a quick shot while his freight was stopped by the brewery.

Franz would always sit by the window and listen to the conversations and watch the people passing in the street. The bartender who looked like John Barrymore in *Svengali* always charged him a quarter less for a drink

than the bartender who looked like Jean Gabin so when
he could Franz bought his drinks from Svengali, whose
name was Tommy.

Even in Port Tropique Franz preferred the poorer
neighborhoods and the company of bums and wondered why after all this time one thing did not matter
very much more than any other.

Death, thought Franz, is the most fascinating thing there is. A friend he'd had in London when he was eighteen, Sullivan Leybourne, had more than anything else in the world wanted to know what it felt like to kill another man. When he was twelve years old, Sullivan had told Franz, he had gone off into the South African bush with nothing but a knife and lived for five days on fruit and insects, sleeping in the boughs of trees, trekking barefoot and alone through the jungle, eluding the search party his parents had dispatched, eventually emerging unscathed and eager for further adventure.

Despite and because of his immature infatuation with death and desire, Sullivan being only slightly older than himself, Franz had liked him immensely. They had shared a flat in Eardley Crescent off the Old Brompton Road in southwest London for several months. Tall, lithe, blond and gray-eyed, Sullivan had been successful with women of all ages, and, due to his calm bravado and carefree ability to spend whatever he had in his pocket on whomever happened to be his companion of the moment, he was a gallant friend to men.

In London as a student purportedly preparing for his Oxford entrance exams, Sullivan, when not in the presence of a lady, a nominal occurrence, spent the early part of the day asleep. He would wake about one, check the post for his allowance, sent weekly from Durban, and proceed to the local Lyons where he would read the newspaper and eat breakfast. The afternoon would usually be spent at the cinema, one of the inexpensive classic theaters, then, for supper, he would visit a girlfriend. Later he would go to a pub or a party, whatever was on hand. His casual and adaptable attitude had never failed to impress Franz in those days.

Sullivan had met a girl named Hannah Muller at a party he went to with Franz. For some time Hannah had utterly consumed him. Sullivan spent all the time he could with her, haunting the corridor outside of the office where she worked, never letting her out of his sight. After a few weeks of this, Sullivan had suddenly stopped seeing her. She asked Franz to tell her what had happened, to ask Sullivan, she had to know, he had given her no explanation.

Sullivan told Franz that he was simply tired of Hannah and didn't know how to tell her. The next time Hannah saw Franz she told him she was going to kill herself. Hannah was a strange girl, with a wild glint in her black eyes and long gray-black hair that made her look older than her thirty-two years. At times she looked ragged and worn, as if she too had spent a lifetime in the mines of Wales, where she had lived until she was twenty. Other days she more resembled a gypsy. She liked to dance alone to Elvis Presley records and imitate Eartha Kitt singing "My Heart Belongs To Daddy."

Franz had thought she might be a bit mad, but not mad enough to do herself in. He had been wrong. She put her head in the gas oven the day after he last saw her. Like in Chaplin's *Limelight* a neighbor found her and pulled her out. However, unlike *Limelight*, she had never recovered.

Sullivan could not blame himself, so he did not. Franz had been shocked and frightened by it all.

"You must admit, man," Sullivan had said to him, "there was always something real about her."

Ivan was the son of the former Viceroy of India. He was born in England but taken to India shortly thereafter where he lived, with occasional holidays back in England, until he was sixteen years old.

He was one of the most proper Englishmen Franz had ever met, extremely well-mannered, never imposing, gracious to the point of frustration. His problem was that he was in love with Franz's girlfriend, who happened to be his ex-wife.

Antoinetta, Franz's girlfriend—Ivan's ex-wife—had first known Ivan in Paris, where they had both been students. He had been in love with her from the start, struck by her incredible beauty, but hopelessly, as she was then involved with her first great love, an American, as was she, also a student, with whom she lived for two years before they broke up. Her boyfriend, Robert, joined the army and was sent to Vietnam. She returned to the States, much to Ivan's dismay.

At least in Paris Ivan was able to see her, follow her around, buy her coffee or lunch when Robert was absent. Antoinetta encouraged admirers, foremost of whom was Ivan, who could look but not touch. She played the Virgin Queen whenever possible, referring to her troupe of suitors as "my sheep" or "my trembling lambs." She was proud of her beauty, having been considered an ugly child, as she told Franz. She craved attention, more than one man could give her, and she had no close relationships with women.

After she had returned to the States, she found she was pregnant by Robert. She wrote him, assuming that he would immediately obtain leave from the service and return to marry her, but she received no answer. She wrote again and again but still received no reply. Finally, in desperation, when she realized Robert had no intention of rescuing her, she began to cast around for a man to legitimize the birth of her child.

Where she lived, in a wealthy, socially-conscious section of Boston, there were few instant prospects, and none whom she cared for enough to share her secret with. As her pregnancy became more evident, she grew increasingly frantic, turning at one point to her eldest half-brother whom she seduced one snowy night in the cockpit of his small plane.

He was as susceptible to her beauty as the others, and eagerly agreed to marry her despite the scandal it would cause. He attempted to fly them that night to Maryland, where her age was acceptable for marriage without parental consent. Almost immediately after takeoff, however, the storm grew worse, and they crashed in a nearby field. Her brother was killed instantly. Antoinetta and the unborn child were unhurt.

This tragedy was soon followed by a letter from Ivan, who was in Dominica working for the British Field Service. He was to be given a holiday, he wrote, and could he visit her? Antoinetta answered affirmatively, by return post. She had her man at last. How could poor Ivan refuse?

He did not, and they were married two weeks after his arrival. He returned to Dominica to finish out his commitment, during which time Antoinetta had the baby. Upon imminent termination of his duty Ivan wrote Antoinetta that he would soon be in Boston. She hastily telegrammed him not to come, that he should go on to London—she would meet him there as soon as she could. Ivan telephoned, protested, but Antoinetta held firm. She would be there, she said, as soon as it was feasible, and Ivan should do as she said. He did.

A year later Antoinetta did come to London, after she had had an affair with a boy in New York, become pregnant again, and had an abortion. She left her child with her mother in Boston.

Once he had her in London Ivan determined to act as her husband, but she would have none of it, told him he was sweet, how grateful she was to him for rescuing her in her hour of need, but that she was not interested in

111

him as a lover, and that she had filed divorce papers before she left Boston.

Ivan was disappointed but he showed her around London, took her to meet his parents, the retired Viceroy and his wife, on their estate in Sussex, and helped her find a place to stay.

A few weeks after her arrival, however, she met Franz, and they were soon living together. Ivan came around fairly often and Franz did not discourage his visits. He liked Ivan and considered him no threat to his relationship with Antoinetta. On the contrary, his presence was often a relief to Franz, as Antoinetta needed more adulation than he was willing to give her. She spoke to Ivan like she could to an intimate woman friend, ask him what stockings or color of lipstick to wear.

Since Franz needed time alone, Antoinetta often felt ignored, and faithful Ivan would supply himself in these situations, accompanying Antoinetta to the cinema or the theatre or on a walk through the park. Ivan fancied himself a journalist but he never held a job for very long. It hardly mattered, though, since he received a sizeable allowance from the old Viceroy.

When Franz and Antoinetta's relationship ran its course, Franz left England and Ivan allowed Antoinetta to move into his flat. Antoinetta and Franz corresponded occasionally during the next two years, and when Franz returned to London for a brief period she met him at the house of an old friend.

She was married, and her daughter Sally was living with them. What about Ivan, Franz asked, what was he doing?

"Oh, Ivan," she said, delightfully. "We wouldn't know what to do without him. He lives with us. He has a room in the attic, takes care of the garden and Sally when Ambrose and I are away."

"Did you ever consider," Franz said, "what you've done to Ivan? He's surrendered his life to you and received nothing in return."

Antoinetta looked hurt.

"Nothing?" she said. "He has me the only way he can, the only way he ever could."

"It's not enough." Franz told her.

Antoinetta smiled.

"It's enough for Ivan," she said.

Franz lay in his bed at the Delicado smoking and waiting for the rain to let up. Nathan was leaving and Franz was to meet him and Joanna Noyes at the Consuelo for a goodbye.

There had been no sign of Renaldo or Rodriguez and he was beginning to think his return to Port Tropique had been unnecessary. He had to decide what to do again.

In the last few days Franz had thought of everyone he had ever known that he could still remember. The common theory is that when you die your entire life passes in front of you during that final instant. If that was true, it seemed to Franz, then he was dying in slow motion.

After Nathan had gotten into a taxi and driven off to the airport, Joanna suggested to Franz that, since it had stopped raining for the moment and the night air was less steamy than usual, they take a walk together. Franz was surprised that she had not left with Nathan and said so.

"How do you mean that?" she asked.

"Everybody else seems to be clearing out," he said. "And I thought you and Paul were getting friendly."

Joanna laughed and stopped to light a cigarette before going on.

"He's too impatient for me."

"Do you mean in general, or are you referring to his sexual habits?"

She looked over at him and smiled, showing Franz as many of her perfect little teeth as possible.

"Both," she said, and they laughed.

"I'm leaving tomorrow by train for Redondo. Since Raoul refuses to grant interviews, *Newsweek* wants a story on Torres.

"I can't say I blame him," said Franz. "The wolves are dying to get at him."

Before Franz realized it they had walked almost to the old dock where the pick-ups and deliveries had been made. Soldiers were patrolling the area and laborers were working by lantern light, laying foundations for housing.

"Raoul isn't wasting any time," Joanna said.

They turned down the beach and Joanna put her arm through Franz's. When they had passed the boundary of light from the construction site she stopped and looked at him and showed her teeth again.

After Franz kissed her she took off her shoes and ran down to the water and splashed around for a bit before coming back. She picked up her shoes, looped an arm through his, and they began walking back toward the light.

"The world's affairs and the floating clouds—why question them?" said Franz.

"Chinese?"

Franz nodded. "Wang Wei."

"Paul said he thought at first you were CIA, but, now he figures you're just looking for a reason to stay alive."

"Why should I be different from anybody else?" Franz asked.

Franz's Uncle Ben, who was not really his uncle, had always done well with the women. That's how he would say it, and he enjoyed talking about his ex-wives and girlfriends. Franz and his friends enjoyed listening, too, because Ben wasn't much of a liar and they figured to learn something. It was already happening, the thing with the women, and Franz wasn't fifteen yet.

Ben rarely told the same story twice and explained how he'd done certain things or the women had done certain things that Franz and his friends couldn't even understand anyone wanting to do. But Ben was not a liar and Franz and the others believed him when he told them they would end up doing these things too, sometimes even if they didn't really want to do them.

"The important thing," Ben said, "is to be nice. If you are nice to the women they will be even nicer to you. That is the way the good women are. If you find that after you are nice to them they are not even nicer to you then you have not got a good woman and you should forget her and find another. That is the second thing to remember, there is always"—he repeated the word—"always another woman. There is always another man for a woman, too," he added, "but that is not usually the same. Usually for a woman there are other men rather than another man and that is not the same."

Franz did not really understand that last part but by then Ben was telling them how he was still friends with all three of his ex-wives and almost all of those girlfriends of his with whom he kept in touch. The reason for that, he said, was because he had always been nice to them and so they stayed nice to him. "An ex-wife or girlfriend who stays your friend can often be the best kind of friend," he said.

Ben told a story about one of the nicest girls he had ever known. He'd met her in the Virgin Islands, he said, and Franz and his friends all laughed. Ben and his business partner had gone there for a fortnight's holiday during the winter a few years before and met this girl on the beach the first day. She was twenty-three years old and was vacationing alone before she went back to Ohio to get married.

Ben and his business partner took her to dinner and that night and for the next ten days she slept with them, swam with them and ate with them. The three of them spent all of their time together and it was wonderful, Ben said. She was perfectly happy with both of them and would even wake them up in the middle of the night to do any of those certain things he had told the boy and his friends about before.

At the end of the ten days Ben and his business partner went back home and the girl went to Ohio. A few weeks later, Ben told the boys, he and his partner each received invitations to her wedding. They didn't go, Ben said, but it showed how things could be if you were nice.

One of Franz's friends told Ben he thought it was pretty hard to be nice to some of the girls he knew, even the ones he would like to do certain things with. Ben said that there were some women it was better not to be nice to but not many and those were not usually the women that really mattered.

Franz asked Ben why he had not stayed married to any of his wives. "They were all nice girls," Ben said, "nice girls. But they wanted too much. They each wanted me to be more of the time a way that I could only be part of the time and no matter how much we did any of the certain things we did or how good it was when we did them it did not mean a thing when it came to their wanting me to be more of the time the way that I could be only part of the time."

Ben looked at him and Franz nodded as if he understood what Ben had said and Ben looked away and started talking about something else.

The National Boxing Championship, sponsored by the Revolutionary Committee, was held in the ballroom of the Hotel Tropique. Alfonso guided Franz through the maze of excited, fatigue-adorned soldiers to seats four rows from the ring, where two barechested, khaki-trousered disciples of socialism were engaged in a valiant struggle to break the other's nose or worse. Whenever the action slowed, the crowd began to jeer and shout insults, accusing the combatants of a dearth of ánimo and cojones.

Alfonso explained to Franz that the tournament was Raoul's idea, an entertainment and reward for the troops as well as an exercise in camaraderie. Mixed in among the military were white-shirted citizens of all types, including, Franz was interested to note, quite a few Indians. Raoul's programs were to include all of the people, and the boxing championship was the first public event for their benefit.

Anyone who signed up could fight, and he stayed in the ring until he lost. Each match was scheduled for three three-minute rounds, but most ended in knockouts. At the moment Franz and Alfonso sat down, an overweight soldier was absorbing a terrible beating at the flashing fists of his much smaller opponent. By the end of the round the fat one's eyes were cut and bleeding so badly that the referee was forced to stop the fight and declare the smaller man the winner. Great cheers and whistles greeted the decision, and as the lightweight strutted around with gloves raised the battered big guy exited the ring to a cacophony of derisive noises.

He was replaced by a very young Indian wearing white trunks, who was about equal in size to the current king. They immediately mixed it up with a frantic flurry of punches and the crowd went wild. Khaki pants flailed sideways while white trunks swooped up, down, around and through with looping Kid Gavilan bolo blows. Within one minute white trunks had put khaki pants away and received a raucous appreciation.

The fighters kept coming, none of them surviving past three bouts, each new champion exulting in plaudits from the audience of frenzied sharks. It was a crazy, improbable event, and for a brief interlude Franz was roused from contemplation of his conundrum.

At the sight of one contestant being banged mercilessly around without interference from the referee, Franz recalled the sight of Emile Griffith pummeling Benny Kid Paret to death, Paret's head propped on a corner ring rope, snapping nearly off from Griffith's lightning onslaught, twenty solid blows to the skull being landed before the fight was stopped. At the weigh-in before that fight, Franz remembered, the Cuban Kid had called Griffith a fairy because of his passion for designing women's hats. Paret's death had left his widow with a mink coat, several small children, and a hundred thousand dollars in debts.

In the front row, surrounded by soldiers armed with automatic weapons, sat Raoul. Bearded and smiling and smoking a cigarette in a long black holder, with his glasses on he looked more like a professor than the commandante of a rebel army. He sedately applauded the efforts of each fighter, and never stopped smiling. Watching him Franz had the feeling that El Presidente was indulging his troops with this exhibition, that he himself did not enjoy the spectacle but had the good political sense to make clearly visible his participation as a true compañero.

Franz did not stay to witness the crowning of the final champion, leaving Alfonso still yelling, ecstatic and sweating as two inelegant young bulls butted and battered one another as befit the spirit of the revolution.

Once he awoke thinking he was in Japan. When he realized he was not, he made tea and thought about the father in Ozu's film *An Autumn Afternoon.* Though a widower he has no choice but to encourage his daughter to marry and begin a life of her own, apart from him and her brother, this despite her spoken reluctance to do so. When finally she marries a man she does not know, and whom Ozu does not show, the look in her eyes convinces the father that she is as horrified by the procedure as he, but they are helpless in the face of convention.

A vision of the daughter's delicate, quiet beauty remained in Franz's mind. Never again, her father knew, would she reflect that exquisite, pristine expression. She would be yet another person, as he, too, had, and would again, become. Franz could imagine no fate more terrible than the inability to accept change, but he felt no link with the future, an emotion, he realized, that had begun irrevocably to erode his objective perception of the past.

Franz's friend Dale had invited him home with him one weekend from college. Dale was a very Southern Baptist St. Louis boy who would have joined the Klan, he told Franz, but for the fact that the FBI would most likely make a record of his membership which could conceivably jeopardize his ever holding public office or working for the government.

When Dale told his parents at the dinner table that Franz was a Catholic, Dale's mother said she had never knowingly eaten dinner with a Catholic before. She had once attended a Methodist Women's luncheon, however, and she supposed that was almost the same thing.

Dale's father worked a six day week at his appliance store and on Sundays, if the weather was good, sat in a flamingo chair in his yard and shot crows. He hated crows, he told Franz, they were cockroaches with wings.

The big event of the weekend had been a Saturday night poker game at the house of an old buddy of Dale's which didn't end until four o'clock Sunday morning. Franz had won the most, about forty dollars, which disturbed Dale greatly. Franz could never get Dale to tell him exactly what upset him so much but after that it was clear their friendship was over.

Back at the university they seldom met, when they did Dale offered no more than a half-look and a mumbled hello, and it wasn't long before Franz had forgotten whatever it was they'd had in common in the first place.

So here I am, he thought, sitting in a stinking little room in a tenth-rate hotel in a banana republic town occupied by a rebel army expecting to be attacked any day. I've got two handguns, five hundred thousand dollars in stolen cash I can't spend in a suitcase under the bed and no place to go where I can do myself any good. If I leave they'll find me and if I stay here long enough a couple of monsters will come through the door and stick a bullet in my ear and take the money without listening to anything I have to say.

If he ever wrote a book, Franz decided, he would put into it everyone he had ever liked or disliked. It would be called *Tragic Creatures*.

Franz left the guns in the room. There was no reason for Raoul to reject his offer. After all, the new government needed money, and half a mill was enough of a shot to impress anybody, even a socialist.

After they had thoroughly gone over both Franz and the suitcase the two guards led him, one in front, one behind, to the service elevator. It opened into the penthouse and there was Raoul, dressed out in fatigues, long black cigarette holder in his mouth, sitting at a large desk littered with guns, cartridge belts and telephones. Raoul looked up through his wire-rim spectacles and studied Franz carefully. The guards stood one on each side of him, leaving Franz alone in front of the desk.

"What do you want in exchange for the money?" Raoul said in English.

"Protection," said Franz.

"From whom?"

"A group of smugglers who've been running phony ivory through here to the Far East. I was their bag man. The night your army took Port Tropique I left with the cash for Tampeche."

"Why did you return?"

'"I figured if I ran they'd find me and kill me. I came back hoping to find them first and tell them I was just trying to protect it during the revolution, that I'd never meant to cop it. But I haven't been able to locate either of the front men I was dealing with. It's been too long, they'd never believe me now, so I need help and I figured you could use the half a millon. It's not doing me any good."

Raoul leaned back in his chair and crossed his legs. He took a cigaret from a pack in his shirt pocket, stuck it into the holder, put it into his mouth and lit it. Franz noticed that through his beard Raoul's lips looked very thin, that quite probably when he smiled he bared his gums.

"What can I do to protect you?"

"'As soon as they're reasonably certain you're in power to stay, they'll contact you in order to make arrangements to continue the operation. When they do, tell them part of the deal is their guarantee that I'll be left unharmed, here or anywhere I go. Until then I want a couple of bodyguards."

"What makes you think I would make a deal with them in the first place?"

"I don't, but they'll offer a lot of money in regular installments. The only other way for me to get out of it is if you catch them all and kill them, and that won't happen. Hitting the front men wouldn't do any good, anyway, and the big guys never show their faces."

Raoul stared at Franz for a few moments, then uncrossed his legs and leaned forward with his elbows on the desk.

"It certainly is a rum situation for you, Señor Hall," he said. "I am sorry, but I cannot spare any of my men for your protection. However, if such contact as you describe is made with my government, in return for your contribution I would do my best to see that, insofar as is possible, your welfare is guaranteed."

"That's the best you'll do?"

"If I chose to I could take the money from you on the basis of a currency violation and, depending on whether the old law or the new law was observed, you could be executed or put in jail. At least you would be protected there."

"All right," said Franz. "But you'll let me know when you're contacted."

"If such a thing occurs I will see that you are informed. Where can you be located?"

"At the Hotel Delicado on Calle Diez y Ocho."

"On behalf of the free republic then, señor, I thank you."

Franz turned to go, then stopped.

"Do you mind if I take the suitcase?" he asked. "It was my grandfather's."

Raoul smiled, but because of the beard Franz could not tell whether or not his gums were bared. "It will be returned to you once the contents have been verified and registered by the Revolutionary Committee."

In The Habana Franz ordered a Noche Buena and a shot of whisky. He poured the whisky into the beer and drank it straight down in several long swallows. It was a very hot day and drinking the boilermaker like that made him dizzy.

If Marie were here, he thought, none of it would matter. Then it occurred to him that the real reason Marie was not with him and never would be was because he was stupid.

Three days after his meeting with Raoul, Franz spotted Renaldo turning the corner into Calle Dos. He followed him into the market and lost him on Huaraches Row, but he was certain it had been the serpent in his white suit and blue-banded panama. This meant the fix was in, otherwise Renaldo wouldn't chance being seen, and Franz headed straight to the Tropique.

At first he couldn't get in, but he persisted, shouting about how he had contributed to the cause, to tell El Presidente he was there. After waiting an hour he was taken into the elevator and up to headquarters. Raoul was speaking into two telephones at the same time and when he hung them up he looked sternly at Franz and asked sharply in clipped Spanish what he wanted now.

"I just saw Renaldo in the street. You must have made a deal with them."

"Con qui? What are you talking about? We have made no deal."

"Renaldo wouldn't show his face unless you'd made an arrangement. Did you tell them to lay off me?"

"Señor Hall, I have not much patience for you today. You will kindly accept that there has been no arrangement of the kind you have mentioned. It must have been someone other than this man Renaldo you saw."

"No, it was him. I'm certain of it."

"Well, senor, there is nothing I can do. Be assured that we will impart to you any information that may be of interest. Now I must say good afternoon."

A guard grasped Franz's arm and led him firmly away.

This is the end, thought Franz, as he walked quickly toward the Delicado. As he passed the Café Roma across from the zócalo he could hear Huey Smith singing "Don't You Just Know It" on the jukebox, and he was suddenly overwhelmed by a desire for barbecued shrimp the way they were served at Blom's in New

Orleans. By the time he reached the hotel he knew it was time to get out once and for all, regardless of the money. Maybe Raoul would fix it for him and he'd be all right, if he didn't then at least he'd die in Dixie.

Franz got a seat on the late flight on Aviatéca Tropicál. The airplane was packed with American reporters and a few others he assumed were either foreign diplomats or oil company executives.

He couldn't relax until the plane had left the ground, and even then did not fully comprehend the fact that in an hour and a half he would be back in the States. He sat in a window seat and did not speak to anyone. He felt ready to pass the rest of his life in silence.

Despite his anxiety, the steady drone of the engines soon put Franz to sleep, and he dreamed it was he instead of Pastor Wunderlich who met Madame Buddenbrook running hatless through the rain to throw herself into the river over the theft of her silver spoons. In the dream he was forced to shoot Sergeant Lenoir and was being pursued by Napoleon's soldiers when he awoke, sweating and confused, just as the plane was landing.

These days the ceiling fans in Blom's provided atmosphere rather than cool breezes, there was air-conditioning for that, but Franz was glad to see them revolving over the customers as if relief from the oppressive southern heat was still their responsibility. The air-conditioning was typical, thought Franz, of the differences between Port Tropique and New Orleans. Both Blom's and The Habana had ceiling fans but in the States there was always something extra.

Franz sat at the long mahogany bar eating barbecued shrimp and drinking cold Beck's. The bar in Blom's was probably his favorite since the black walnut bar that was in The Sea Breeze restaurant in Tampa had been sold to a private citizen before the building was torn down.

He had finished the last of the shrimps, rinsed his fingers in warm lemon water, and ordered another beer when Joanna Noyes walked in with two men in tan suits. The bar was next to the entrance and Joanna saw Franz right away and rushed over and kissed him.

"Well hello!" she said. "I certainly didn't expect to run into you! What are you doing here?"

"The usual," said Franz. "Looking for a reason to stay alive. How about you? The last I remember you were going off in search of General Torres."

"Oh I found the pig, and stuck him too. He even made the cover." She spread her hands in front of her face like a headline. " 'Fascists Fight Back!' Didn't you see the article?"

Franz shook his head no.

"Anyway, I'm working out of New Orleans now, at least for a while. Are you staying?"

"For a while."

Joanna looked for the two men she'd come in with and found them sitting at a table against the wall.

"I've got an apartment on Governor Nicholls Street," she said, taking a pen and pad from her purse.

She wrote down her address and phone number and gave the paper to Franz.

"Call me, all right?"

"Yes. Say, have you heard anything from Nathan?"

"He's in Africa. Ethiopia, I think, with the Eritreans."

Franz nodded and smiled.

"That ought to make him happy."

"Do you want to meet my friends?"

"No, I'll see you another time."

Joanna kissed him.

"Soon," she said.

Franz nodded and she went to join the men.

He finished his beer, paid the check and stood up to go, glancing over at Joanna. She was talking away and one of the men had an arm around her. Franz caught her eye and she waved and blew him a kiss and he waved back and went out.

Wandering around the city again Franz was surprised at how much he had missed it. He had forgotten how many beautiful black women there were in New Orleans, a fact he mentioned to Joanna two nights later in her apartment, to which she had invited him for dinner.

"Come to think of it," Joanna said, "I haven't seen many really good-looking white women in New Orleans. Why is that?"

"I don't know, but the real southern white beauties seem to come from Atlanta. Before porno films became a legitimate major industry, whenever you saw one with a lot of beautiful girls in it you could bet it had been made in Atlanta. All the southern small town high school cheerleaders and beauty queens who wanted to be movie stars and couldn't afford a ticket to Hollywood flocked to Atlanta and wound up making loops.

"It's still the big business city down here. New Orleans, along with Charleston, and maybe Savannah, have always had a different feeling about them. They're still a bit down-home and, if you're white, comfortably archaic, unlike Atlanta, which is the 'progressive' south, as it's called now, or the 'new' south, which I take to mean any cracker town with a skyline that looks like a cardboard cut-out."

After dinner Joanna and Franz went around the corner to a mostly gay bar on St. Ann called Dreamland. Franz told her about Tujague's and she made him promise to take her there. Then they went back to her apartment and went to bed.

In the middle of the night Joanna shook Franz awake.

"What's the matter?" he asked.

"You were yelling. 'He's my son, he's my son,' you kept saying."

"I'm sorry," said Franz, putting his arm around Joanna and kissing her. "Go back to sleep."

"Do you want to tell me about it?"

"Not now."

"Franz?"

"Yeah?"

"You're *not* CIA, are you?"

Franz got up, got dressed, and left the apartment without saying anything.

The bartender in Dreamland reminded Franz of Alan Ladd, the way he looked in *Shane*. One rainy afternoon in Tokyo Franz had taken Marie to see *Shane* at a neighborhood movie house, after first making sure it was not a dubbed version. Except for a column of characters on the right hand side of the screen that resembled chicken tracks, the print of the film had been practically pristine.

Seeing a sentimental movie like *Shane* in Tokyo was bizarre in that it brought back to Franz a series of childhood memories, including the death of his father, who had taken him to see it when Franz was about eight years old. Franz had sat there in the movie theater in the middle of Japan crying, watching the boy run after Alan Ladd shouting, "Shane, come back!" It had occurred to Franz then how inexorable life was, and he'd been overwhelmed. Death hadn't made sense to him when he was a boy, and the fact that it suddenly and violently did was no less bewildering.

Franz loved a story he'd heard about Joe DiMaggio and Marilyn Monroe. It made him feel less guilty about his part in the relationship with Marie.

Joe D. and Marilyn were still married, he'd recently retired from baseball, and he went to meet her at the airport, where she was returning from a tour of Army bases in Korea.

"Oh Joe," she gushed, streaking the Yankee Clipper's cheek with her red mouth, golden head blowing wild in the San Francisco wind, "you never heard such cheering!"

"Yes I have," said Joe.

Franz's money was beginning to run low, so he moved to a cheap room above a movie theater on Elysian Fields. He passed the days sitting and looking at the river and the nights reading paperback novels that he bought for a dime and re-sold for a nickel at a thrift store on Magazine Street. He did not see Joanna Noyes. Somebody else would have to take her to Tujague's, he decided.

One afternoon he noticed that the movie theater he lived above was showing *The Westerner* with *The Wild Bunch*, so he went in. He sat down just as Gary Cooper woke up in the arms of Walter Brennan. Brennan, who in the film was portraying Judge Roy Bean, reminded Franz of a seedy version of Max Kroner, and he found himself thinking about Kroner throughout the show.

It was true what the professor in The Habana had said about it being unusual that Kroner's wife had stuck by him. Not that Marie could have been expected to act differently than she had. Max Kroner had been a lucky man, that's all.

Franz looked up to see William Holden, Warren Oates, Ben Johnson and Ernest Borgnine in slow motion slaughtering and being slaughtered by dozens of Mexican soldiers, and then the moronic bounty hunters picking over their bodies like buzzards. At the end Robert Ryan, the former buddy of the wild bunch who'd been forced by the cops to track them down, joins the old bandit Edmond O'Brien and his Mexican crony and rides off in the desert, the last of a kind, with nothing to look forward to.

Outside the theater the sky was hazy and not quite dark. When Franz spotted Renaldo in the car he walked toward him slowly and didn't see Rodriguez's gun until the instant before it fired.

About the Author

BARRY GIFFORD was born in Chicago, Illinois in 1946, and was raised there and in Florida. He has lived in London and San Francisco, among other places, and worked as a merchant seaman, musician, truck driver and journalist. He is the author of numerous books of poetry and fiction, including the novel *Landscape with Traveler* and the fictional memoir *A Good Man To Know*. He is also coauthor, with Lawrence Lee, of major biographies of Jack Kerouac and William Saroyan. Mr. Gifford has been the recipient of the Maxwell Perkins Award from PEN, a National Endowment for the Arts Fellowship in Creative Writing for Fiction, and a PEN Syndicated Fiction Prize. He presently lives in Northern California.